PRAISE FOR
TWICE DYING

"Devastating. . . . *Twice Dying* is a genuinely frightening and suspenseful thriller that demands to be read in one sitting. Neil McMahon surely has a future of prestige and honor ahead of him."
The Missoulian

"A wild plot . . . Satisfying . . . Reads like a cross between Raymond Chandler and Thomas Harris. More Monks, please, Mr. McMahon."
Chicago Tribune

"McMahon tells a story that is rich in medical detail and steeped in horror."
San Antonio Express News

TWICE DYING

NEIL McMAHON

HarperTorch
An Imprint of HarperCollins*Publishers*

For Kim

This is a work of fiction. Names, characters, places, and incidents are products of the author's imagination or are used fictitiously and are not to be construed as real. Any resemblance to actual events, locales, organizations, or persons, living or dead, is entirely coincidental.

HARPERTORCH
An Imprint of HarperCollins*Publishers*
10 East 53rd Street
New York, New York 10022-5299

First HarperTorch paperback printing: November 2000
First HarperCollins hardcover printing: March 2000

HarperCollins®, HarperTorch™, and ❦™ are trademarks of HarperCollins Publishers Inc.

Printed in the United States of America

Visit HarperTorch on the World Wide Web at www.harpercollins.com

❖ 10 9 8 7 6 5 4 3 2 1

Acknowledgments

This book owes a great debt to help from many people. Special thanks to:

Kim Anderson, Dan Betz, Constance Chang, Carl Clatterbuck, Dan Conaway, Alix Douglas, Frances Kuffel, Drs. Barbara and Dan McMahon, and Dr. Dick Merriman.

Thanks also to the Wallace Stegner Fellowship Program at Stanford University, and to the Fine Arts Work Center in Provincetown, Massachusetts, for providing support in the past; and to the Jean Naggar Literary Agency, for their sterling efforts.

Now the serpent was more subtil than any beast of the field which the Lord God had made.

—Genesis 3:1

Prologue

Francis Jephson pushed the video cassette into his office VCR and sat while the screen came to life. The film began abruptly. It was silent, grainy, amateurish, with dim, even lighting. The camcorder, stationary, looked down on a room of rough stone, wet in patches from seeping water, curving up to form a high-ceilinged vault. The far walls faded into deeper blackness.

In the foreground, a man lay on the floor. He was unconscious, his face flattened, mouth slightly open, giving him a fishlike look. His face was abraded, as if he had been dragged. A red baseball cap was set on his head.

Jephson knew him. His name was Caymas Schulte.

Caymas began to move, face twitching, eyelids flickering. He grimaced, one thick hand going to his cheek to touch the raw skin. He rose to an elbow, then heaved himself to his knees, but something yanked him back. His groping fingers found it: a tether around his neck, a horse's rein of heavy leather. He turned to where it led and stared.

The tether was knotted to a skeletal iron rack, the type used in warehouses. A dozen similar tethers were knotted in a horizontal line beside his, a few feet apart. All hung, severed, trailing lifelessly on the floor. Above each was mounted a white oval: plaster masks of men's faces, their features contorted with struggle.

Above Caymas Schulte's place there was no mask, but a white heap of plaster on a board. He reached out to touch it. His finger sank in.

He twisted suddenly in clumsy panic. A figure lunged toward him, a dark blur: slender, agile, covered from neck to foot in tight-fitting black. Its arm slashed downward, severing the rein.

Caymas threw himself backward, flailing and kicking. He rolled away and scrambled to his feet, then backed toward the room's far walls, lips forming silent words of threat or plea. The figure followed, crouched, gliding. The face was visible now: a chalk-white oval, like a mime's, with blood-red rings around the eyes. Dark hair streamed down past the shoulders.

The gloved right hand held a knife that ended in a short, hooked blade.

The screen went blank. Several seconds later, a different image appeared.

Jephson watched without moving or changing expression until his desk phone rang. He picked it up.

"Dr. Jephson?" his secretary said. "John Garlick is here for his appointment."

In a crisp British accent, Jephson said, "Just a moment."

He switched off the television and waited until the screen died. "All right. Send him in."

The door to his outer office opened. Two men were standing just outside. The first was white, in his mid-thirties, wearing gray hospital pajamas. His thick dark hair was brushed back in a spiky mane. He was well built and handsome except for a hardness to his eyes.

Behind him stood a much larger, black, security guard, armed with nightstick, handcuffs, and radio.

"Thank you, Harold," Jephson said to the guard. "Shall we say, forty-five minutes?"

Harold nodded and stepped back, closing the door.

"Sit down, John."

Garlick walked forward with a hint of swagger, his mouth relaxing into a smirk, and sat.

Jephson leaned forward across the desk, lacing his fingers together, and said, "Let's talk about your release."

1

The emergency room at San Francisco's Mercy Hospital was mid-range, with fifteen beds and Level II trauma capability, equipped to handle whatever came through the doors as long as there was not too much of it at once.

Business was usually brisk, and the general degree of tension moderate. Death was not common, although when it did come it tended to happen quickly.

This was a fact that Carroll Monks never lost sight of.

The evening had been crisis-free, and Monks was allowing himself a break, in the faint hope that things would stay that way. His gaze caught the raised hand of Leah Horvitz, the ER's charge nurse, beckoning him. He walked to the admitting desk.

"A woman just left a phone message for you," Leah said. "She asked you to go look in your car."

"*In* my car? My car is locked, Mrs. Horvitz."

"I'm just repeating the message."

"That's all? She didn't leave a name?"

"She said you'd know."

"Did she *hit* my vehicle?"

"If she did, Doctor, I'm sure she came out second best."

Monks caught grins on the faces of staff within hearing range.

"I'll ignore that, Mrs. Horvitz. All right. I'll be back in a minute."

It was a damp night, mid-November, with fog rolling in, high thin clouds that might or might not burn off with tomorrow's sun. Monks walked through the parking lot with vague apprehension, possibilities turning in his mind: a prank, a setup for a mugging, a disgruntled patient who had planted a bomb. His vehicle, a 1974 Ford Bronco made of old-fashioned Detroit iron and the heart of a Percheron, was parked in the physicians' section. As usual, the nearby Saabs and Lexuses had given it a wide berth. There were no signs of a collision.

But a white gift box, a little bigger than a deck of cards, rested on the driver's seat.

Monks tried the door. It was locked, the way he had left it.

He turned slowly, his gaze searching the parking lot. There were no other human beings in sight.

He opened the door and cautiously picked up the box. It had a good weight, the feel of something solid. He scanned the parking lot again, then took off the lid.

Inside was an antique straight razor. Its smooth-worn ivory handle was inlaid with a silver caduceus: the winged staff with two entwined snakes, symbol of the medical profession. It was easy to imagine as a prized possession of a doctor from an older generation.

Easier yet to think of the only other person who still had keys to things of his.

Six years ago, a psychologist named Alison Chapley had been called in to consult on a case with a malpractice insurance group which Monks worked for as expert witness/consultant/investigator. She was very attractive, very sharp, and more than ten years younger than he. The richness and promise of her life seemed apparent, and it never occurred to him that she might see him as anything but an amusing curmudgeon.

One Friday afternoon, he had walked out of the company's offices on Montgomery Street and found Alison waiting, leaning back against the building in a pose he would come to know well, one hand cupping the other elbow, cigarette held between two fingers.

He said, "Could I give you a ride someplace?"

"I think you're a cripple, Dr. Monks."

Monks blinked in astonishment, then set his jaw. "Is that a free diagnosis, Dr. Chapley?"

"It's never free. What do you like?"

"I'm not sure what you mean."

"You know what I mean." She pushed away from the wall and handed him a business card with an address hand-written on back. "Drop by. Tomorrow would be fine."

Her house was near Bolinas, secluded from its neighbors, on a low bluff overlooking the Pacific. Her car was there, but she did not answer the door. Monks hesitated, but then stepped inside and walked through, calling her name. A pair of French doors opened onto a deck. He saw that she was sunbathing in a lounge chair, her back to him.

He did not realize she was nude until he said hello, and she leaped to her feet, gasping, hands flying to cover herself.

Monks said, "You shouldn't leave your door unlocked. Anybody could come walking in."

Beneath the sheen of oil she was flushed—vibrant, he would realize later, from the drug XTC.

"I like surprises," she said, and let her hands fall to her sides.

Alison had surprised him many times after that: sometimes by leaving a gift in his vehicle. He began to glean that each one had a significance that only she understood. A photograph. A book. A spike-heeled shoe.

A black silk scarf, embroidered with gold.

The parking lot's argon lights, blurred and diffused by fog, colored the night a garish pink-orange, bringing to mind his ticket home from eight months of war: falciparum malaria, tiny mosquito-borne protozoa that invaded the liver and burst forth to storm the bloodstream, killing a million human beings per year and forcing fevered delirium on hundreds of millions more.

He remembered his last vision of Alison, burned into his mind through a fierce haze of vodka on a night he could almost believe was one of those hallucinations: his hands tightening that scarf around her throat, urging her slowly and not ungently to the floor beneath him, with her choked sounds that might have been fear, or pleasure, or laughter. That had been five years ago. He had not seen her or spoken to her since.

Monks gazed into the night with the dense weight of the razor clasped in his palm, rubbing the smooth ivory between thumb and forefinger, as if it were a talisman that could help him see into the reason behind this new offering.

He was still standing there when a hospital attendant came running out of the ER.

"City Triage Base is on the phone, Doctor. You better hurry."

Monks tossed the razor into the Bronco's glove compartment, and ran.

Leah Horvitz was working the phone at the Mobile Intensive Care station, the hospital's contact with paramedics in the field. The tension in her face brought him a jolt of adrenaline. He automatically noted the time, 8:47 P.M., and waited beside her, gathering information from the questions she asked into the phone. Within a minute, he had most of the story.

The Saturday Night Knife and Gun Club had just held a meeting in the Mission District. The result had been a gangfight, or, in official parlance, a "multiple casualty incident." The main Level I Trauma Center at SF General was even more of a zoo than usual. The spillover was being farmed out by the city's triage base to other area hospitals, whether they wanted it or not.

"We're getting two," Leah said, hanging up the phone. "One critical, gunshots to chest and abdomen. The other not critical, shot in the thigh. They think it was automatic weapons. ETA nine minutes."

Monks glanced at the faces of the people in the waiting room. They were going to have to keep waiting.

He turned to scan the ER, envisioning the movements of personnel and gurneys as they would come in, constructing a mental flow chart of probabilities. It was a good guess that the slugs were nine millimeter, which seemed to be the round of choice among the rapid-fire crowd these days. It was also likely that they were lead, which tended to deform and stop within the body. Jacketed rounds were more likely to exit, in which case the chest wound would be on his way to a different institution.

High-powered lead slugs in chest and belly. This was going to be quick and nasty.

His gaze settled on his resident, a lanky straw-haired North Dakota farmboy with the singular name of Vernon Dickhaut, who was sitting across the room on a gurney, one leg swinging, absorbed in a chart.

Monks said, "I want Dr. Dickhaut to take this. Report to him, please." He followed Leah's scurrying walk to Vernon, who glanced up with his trademark expression of bewilderment: a look suggesting that he had just been bashed with a two-by-four.

Monks said to him, "You're in charge until one of us says different. Leah?"

She went into a rapid rundown of the incoming situation. Vernon set down the clipboard, his startled blue eyes widening further.

"The critical's got trouble breathing and low blood pressure," she said. "Gained twelve points with MAST suit inflation." She stopped talking. Vernon's gaze moved to Monks. Monks stared back impassively, arms folded.

Vernon was on rotation, had been in the ER

just two months, and had some experience handling trauma, but never anything like this. Monks could see the realization starting in his face that he was going to be literally holding a life in his hands with minutes or even seconds to save it, that a slip or hesitation could make the difference.

Monks said, "You don't have to do this."

Vernon's shoulders shifted toward the wide glass double doors, where in approximately seven minutes an ambulance would arrive to unload its bloody cargo.

"I'll do it."

"Good. Think out loud."

"I see two immediate problems." Vernon spoke hesitantly, with the care of a schoolboy at the state spelling bee. "The critical's losing blood fast. Maybe a clipped artery."

"In his chest? Belly?"

"I'm guessing belly. If he had a chest cavity full of blood, there'd be other signs."

"Second problem?"

"His breathing. Sounds like a lung's been hit."

Monks allowed him a nod. The MAST suit, Military Anti-Shock Trousers, compressed bleeding vessels and maximized circulation. The suit's inflation had increased blood pressure, which probably meant a damaged artery; if it was in the chest, there would have been other signs, from hacking up great bloody gouts to immediate death.

"What about the other guy, the thigh wound?"

"He's not critical. We make him comfortable and get to him later."

"Go on."

"You did a lot of this, didn't you?" Vernon said. "Gunfire." He pulled nervously on his large fingers.

Monks understood the unspoken plea for help and relented another notch. Guessing at the damage was one thing. Knowing where to start was another.

"I'd assume the blood loss is stabilized and worry instead about his breathing," Monks said. "Ever done a chest tube?"

"Once, in dog lab."

"Same procedure, Vernon," Monks said kindly. "The stakes are higher. Mrs. Horvitz is waiting for orders. I'll meet you in the trauma room in three minutes."

Monks stayed long enough to hear Vernon's hurried instructions to Leah—bring in lab and X-ray, alert the OR, full cart in the trauma room with all personnel standing by. Then Monks walked through the ER, the kind of one-minute scan that told him without conscious thought most of what was going on: which cubicles were open and closed, patients' appearances, positions of the nurses, whether clipboards on the desk had blank charts or lab results and EKGs. His ears picked up a bedside pump measuring medication into an IV, a child's cry, the hiss of an automatic blood pressure cuff. The room was stirring in an

imperceptibly different way now. Staff were
moving with the kind of hushed speed used
around patients who were already scared and
about to be a lot more so.

Monks stepped into the trauma room. The
cart was already there, brought by a nurse who
was young and relatively new to the unit: Jackie,
he recalled. It took him a moment to supply the
last name: Lukas. She was lean-faced, with sandy
hair pulled back in a ponytail; not pretty, but
attractive in an athletic sort of way. She smiled
nervously and murmured a greeting. He had
worked directly with her only a few times, and
not in crisis. There was no telling how she would
hold up. With Vernon, that made two unknowns.
Monks decided to make sure Leah Horvitz was
nearby when the action started.

He glanced over the cart's equipment and
adjusted the overhead light as he spoke.

"Lay out a suture set and a couple of chest
tubes, thirty-three French. Gowns, goggles, two
pair of gloves apiece. Seven and a half for me. Dr.
Dickhaut's are probably bigger." He noted that
she moved quickly and without questions, a good
sign.

Vernon entered, and all three stepped into
plastic barrier gowns, mandatory trauma apparel
in the age of AIDS. Monks caught Vernon's eye
and held up a second pair of gloves. The trick was
one a nervous resident might or might not
remember. The outer pair could be stripped off

after the exterior body examination, leaving the inner gloves sterile for going in without pausing to reglove. It could save as much as twenty seconds. He stepped to the door and looked at the clock. It was 8:58. The ambulance was a minute late.

Then he caught the rumble of an approaching vehicle and backup beeper, quickly growing louder. As many times as he had heard it, it still brought a rush. There was no other sound quite like it.

Flashing lights moved in to sweep the room, pulsing reds and blues from the ambulance and squad cars. Personnel crowded through the door. Alarmed patients edged away, staring. Monks walked back to Vernon, who was standing still and pale, and gripped his upper arm hard.

" 'Gird up now thy loins like a man,' " Monks said, " 'for I will demand of thee.' "

The critical came in fast on a gurney wheeled by paramedics, looking like a captured creature out of a science fiction movie: strapped with nylon webbing to a backboard, head taped down and neck pinned by a cervical collar, shirt ripped off his blood-soaked torso, the bright orange MAST pants ballooning around his body. Bags of saline fluid hooked to the gurney's rack dripped through IVs into each arm. He was moving feebly, blood bubbling between his lips. Vernon strode beside him, leaning over, fingers examining head and mouth.

"I'm a *doctor*, you understand me? You're in a hospital, you've been *shot*."

The boy mumbled something. He was slight, olive-skinned, perhaps sixteen, with eyes like a scared fawn's. Monks felt his professional insulation slipping.

The next gurney was trundling in now, flanked by three blue-uniformed SFPD cops. This boy was older, also strapped down, but struggling and panting. A field dressing covered his left leg from hip to knee. The bandage was blood-crusted, but with no sign of an open major vessel.

Monks called, "Five milligrams morphine, IV," to a waiting nurse, then pointed the gurney to the next cubicle.

"We're gonna take *care* of you. Can you breathe, does it hurt?" Vernon was yelling now, leaning close to the first boy. No words came from the mouth: only a raspy unintelligible sound of forced air.

Vernon said, "Airway first."

"Blood loss?"

"No exit wounds and no pumping bleeders. His heart's probably not hit. We've got to trust the MAST suit and IVs."

"Keep moving and keep talking."

Vernon thrust his fingers into the open mouth, probing the upper throat. Sweat glistened on his forehead above his goggles.

"Airway's clear. Let's move him."

The paramedics lifted the backboard onto the

trauma room's stainless steel table. Vernon's fingers traveled over the bloodcaked rib cage, searching for entrance wounds. They paused at a small hole above the right nipple. His hand went flat and moved around the chest, fingers of the other hand tapping its back.

"Right side's hyperresonant. Percussion dullness of the heart has shifted left."

"Check his larynx."

Vernon's fingers moved over it. When he looked up again, the respect in his eyes was evident.

"Displaced left," he said. "I'd say we've got a tension pneumo."

Monks had been reasonably sure of that from the paramedics' description. He had seen a number of them, some from nine-millimeter rounds. Air escaped from a punctured lung and got trapped in the chest cavity, the wound sealed off by the pleural membrane. Pressure held that lung collapsed and useless, while the other functioned with difficulty.

"Proceed."

Jackie said, "Anesthetic?" She was hanging right in there, Monks noted approvingly, hip to hip with Vernon.

Vernon hesitated, then said, "No time."

Monks nodded once more, and Jackie took the chest tube from its sterile wrapping: eighteen inches of plastic one-half inch in diameter, to be pushed through an incision in the rib cage deep into the lung.

A commotion was rising outside, shouting voices coming closer. A blue uniform moved by fast. Monks stepped to the door. A small crowd had formed near the Nurses' Station, the police facing off several young Hispanic men wearing baggy pants and baseball caps turned backward. Limbs flailed in hot gestures, and words flew in staccato street Spanish. He got a brief unsettling flash of being back in Saigon, surrounded by small intense people whose language and intentions he could not understand, except that they might at any second erupt into violence.

A clerk was talking rapidly on the phone, probably to security. Monks glanced back into the trauma room. Vernon was washing the boy's chest with sterile prep solution. It would not be long now, and without anesthesia this was going to get loud. Monks strode to the nearest cop, a burly man with a deeply lined face and organ-grinder mustache. The cop's name tag read SAL-VATORE. He nodded curtly to Monks, his angry gaze staying on one of the young men.

"Says he's the kid's brother," Salvatore said.

"There's a conference room off the main lobby," Monks said. "Have them wait there, and tell them somebody will come talk to them in a few minutes."

The brother's glare shifted to Monks, and he postured, one shoulder thrust forward and other fist clenched. His hair was bristly on top and slicked back on the sides, falling to his shoulders. He was not much over five feet tall.

"He dies, man, you going *with* him, mother-fucker!"

Monks leaned close to his face.

"Your brother can't breathe and his belly's full of blood. You want to come help?"

He watched the eyes turn uncertain and saw through to the truth of it: this was a kid, too, and scared.

But a kid who had likely been part of the incident, who might have pulled a trigger himself, who could threaten death with chilling ease. Monks's own anger and fear bristled as he wheeled and stalked back.

He stepped into the trauma room in time to see Vernon making a scalpel incision low on the right armpit. With a quick glance at Monks, Vernon set aside the scalpel, chose a Kelly clamp, and eased it into the slit, twisting downward. Monks gripped his wrist, stopping him. An artery and nerve ran beneath each rib, vulnerable to the clamp's sharp jaws.

"On *top* of the rib. The artery."

Vernon closed his eyes in despair.

"Shake it off," Monks said fiercely, fingers digging into Vernon's wrist. "Come on, he's dying." Vernon inhaled, readjusted the clamp, then stopped again. His face was almost white. Monks counted, one, two, and just as he was about to shove in and take over, Vernon found his nerve and thrust the clamp through the pleura.

The hiss of escaping air was drowned by the boy's cry, a feeble shriek like the rending of rusted metal. His limbs thrashed against the webbing while Jackie held him down, —but he was breathing again. Vernon, still ashen-faced but now firm, probed the incision with his finger, then slowly introduced the tube into the heaving chest cavity in an obscene parody of sword-swallowing. It would be sewed into place and taped airtight, then attached to a water-seal mechanism to suck out the excess air and allow the lung to expand fully.

Monks glanced up and saw Charlie Kolb, a wiry man with the grim look trauma surgeons developed, standing at the door.

"The OR's here," Monks said to Vernon. "Blood pressure's holding and he's breathing. Get that tube hooked up and we'll call him stable for now."

Kolb was a compendium of nervous gestures, pulling at his ears and lips, running his hand over his thin hair as Monks briefed him. There remained the matter of at least three liters of lost blood, much of it probably sloshing around inside the belly. But the real danger would come with the MAST suit's deflation: whatever damaged blood vessels it was compressing would open again rapidly.

"We'll go into his belly now if you want," Monks said. "Your call."

"Let's get him upstairs. We'll try to clamp him off."

Monks watched with a mixture of letdown and relief as the process of transfer began: the ER's responsibility was ending, the OR's beginning. Surgery was better equipped to handle it, but both of them understood that this was a bad situation for surprises.

The burly cop, Salvatore, was standing outside the next cubicle. One of his partners had moved to the ER entrance and stood with radio in hand, watching the parking lot.

"We think you just got cruised," Salvatore said. "A car came around, bunch of kids; took off when they saw the units. Maybe the other gang, coming by to clean up."

Automatic weaponfire in the ER, Monks thought. Their little hospital was growing up.

"Any idea who or what?"

Salvatore shrugged. "Turf war. The others were Asians. The way they do it now, they leave their wounded and take off; they know we'll bring them to the hospital. Then both sides say it was a drive-by." He nodded at the second boy, lying strapped to his backboard. "We know these guys, they're homeboys. The other kid's an Esposito, with the mouthy brother. This one's Vasquez, Rafael. Rafael ain't talking, he's a tough guy. Got to protect his good buddies that left him bleeding on the sidewalk."

This boy looked older, muscular but slack and

silent now from the morphine, or perhaps because the reality of the situation was starting to break through to him.

"Right, tough guy?" Salvatore said. "How old are you? I want to know, is it gonna be juvie hall or Q?"

The lips moved, a reflexive mutter Monks understood without hearing: *chinga tu madre*.

Salvatore grimaced. "Truth is, he'll be out in a few months. Big reputation and a scar to brag on."

"Give me a minute with him," Monks said, and stepped to the bedside. "The pain coming back?" Rafael Vasquez said nothing, but Monks saw the answer in the glazed defiance of his eyes.

"How's he doin', man?" Rafael's head gestured in the direction of the next room.

"He's not doing too well, Rafael," Monks said quietly. "Tell me something. I'm a doctor, not a cop. I won't rat you off. I just want to understand. What happened that was worth this?"

The eyes went veiled, the head rolling away: all the answer Monks was going to get.

He supposed it was a lesson of history, ethnic groups in a melting pot where the melting was too slow for their liking. In the Mission, the older Mexican and black gangs had kept things relatively stable, but now they were under fierce pressure from immigrant Central Americans, Vietnamese, Taiwanese pushing out from Chinatown, and their own young. Throw in a few eye-watering spices—crack, crank, ice—and readily available weapons from Uzis to bazookas, and what you had was increasingly close to open warfare. In Monk's boyhood on Chicago's south side, tough guys fought with fists, really hard cases carried switchblades or chains, and a few zip guns were rumored. There was also an archaic concept known as "fighting fair."

"I'll get you something for the pain," Monks said. He stepped out of the room, wanting a drink himself.

The ER was settling down, a sort of post-coital lull in the wake of crisis. Outside the lobby entrance, the dark figure of the patrolling officer moved through the night's thickening fog. The Esposito boy's gurney was rolling out of the ER, pushed by two attendants with a nurse alongside, on its way to surgery like a ship sailing off on a long journey: six inches of tube protruding from the chest, oxygen mask over the face, water-seal apparatus and IV bags hanging on the rails, and a cardiac monitor between the feet. The trauma room's inside was littered with bloody debris, wrappings, used instruments, and trays. Vernon and Jackie, spattered with blood and body fluids, goggles pushed up on foreheads, stood like the survivors of a bombing raid.

"The kid next door's had five milligrams of morphine IV," he told Jackie. "Get him five more, please. Clean him up and see if X-ray can locate that slug." To Vernon he said, "His brother's waiting in the conference room. Scared, very hostile. That's part of the job, too."

They both looked tense and exhausted: puzzled, as if not quite grasping that after all that had happened, their work might end wrong, that the giddiness of saving a life might still be shattered by the helplessness of losing it.

Monks said, "You might want to know it was nineteen minutes from entry to surgery. There was nothing—zero—more we could have done. You two were right there."

"I lost it," Vernon said. His head bowed to stare down into his large hands, as if they had dropped the winning touchdown pass.

Sharp annoyance hit Monks at the thought that Vernon was more concerned with his performance than with the patient.

"If I had any complaints, Doctor," Monks said, "believe me, you'd hear them."

He left, already regretting his tone. But Vernon's mind would be off it soon enough, explaining to a young man pumped full of enraged machismo that in order for his little brother to live out the next hour, everything was going to have to go just right.

Monks stripped off gloves and gown and washed with automatic precision. His own scrubs were soaked with sweat and God knew what else, but his shift was almost over. He reported to the Nurses' Station.

"If there's nothing urgent, I'm going to start on my charts," he told Leah.

"There's someone here to see you."

"Mrs. Horvitz, last time I looked, there was a whole roomful of people here to see me. I'd like to think that's because of my charming personality, but I suspect otherwise. Dr. Dickhaut will be available in a few minutes."

"I think it might be the lady who called earlier."

Leah's usual concerned look was gone, replaced by something softer. Perhaps a trifle arch. Appraising.

Monks walked to the glass door of the waiting room. A woman stood just on the other side. She was wearing jeans, boots, and a leather jacket over a sweater. Chin-length chestnut hair. Slim but not willowy, shoulders suggesting strength. Wide mouth, high strong cheekbones, hazel eyes that sloed toward the exotic.

Alison Chapley said, "When are you going to get off the firing line, Rasp?"

The nickname was short for Rasputin. He had picked it up in the navy. Only a few people called him by it anymore. He realized that he was braced in the doorway, as if his body had stopped itself on its way toward her and was holding on to safety.

He said, "I keep trying."

"Are those boys going to be all right?"

"One of them."

"If you're too busy, I'll leave."

Headlights arced into the parking lot. Monks watched, remembering that a carload of possibly armed young men had been sighted earlier. But the vehicle was a newish minivan, not a likely ride for a street gang.

He said, "Too busy for what?"

"It's complicated." She glanced around at the other faces in the waiting room, and Monks had the sudden sense that they were pressing close, listening covertly. "Could I buy you a drink?"

"What's wrong with here?"

Her fingers touched his arm. "Please."

The minivan's occupants were getting out, a woman helping a heavy man who moved with a hand pressed to his flank, lifting his right foot mincingly. Appendix, sciatica, maybe kidney stones: nothing Vernon couldn't handle by himself.

Monks said, "I'm due off at ten. I could meet you."

"Zack's?"

Monks nodded.

"Thanks for the gift," he said. "It's classy."

"I found it in an antique store. I thought of you right off."

"Why a razor?"

She smiled. "I don't know, exactly. It just seemed right. Maybe something about an edge."

Monks watched her walk away, hips swinging, bootheels clicking on the pavement. He turned back inside to find Leah's gaze still on him, as if she could see into his memory.

2

A lison was sitting at the near end of the bar
when Monks walked in. He was not surprised to see a man standing next to her, leaning
against the rail, talking. The man's hand rested
familiarly on her shoulder.

Monks stepped to her other side. She turned
to him quickly, shrugging off the hand as if it
were a suddenly discovered annoyance. The man
glanced at Monks, a sour look that stopped just
short of belligerence, and drank from his beer
bottle.

The place had the feel of a saloon, with a pool
table, a country juke box, and a bandstand that
offered bluegrass on Friday and Saturday nights.
The clientele was mostly male, fit young men
wearing tight jeans and work shirts. In gay San

Francisco, Zack's was straight and determined to show it.

"I'm buying," she said. "Is it still vodka?"

"It is. But not now." Monks had debated the issue on the drive here. He wanted a drink fiercely, but a single drink had never done him any good, and there remained the residual business of the ER charts to finish and patients who were still in some way his.

She pushed a key ring toward him. Monks recognized a large Ford key, to the Bronco, and a worn older one: the key to his house.

"I thought you might want these back," she said.

He left them untouched on the bar. "I might."

She laughed. "I'm out of practice sparring."

"Best I can recall, you never had much competition."

"Not in a place like this." Her voice was loud enough for the man behind her to hear.

Monks gripped her wrist tightly. Her smile faded.

He said, "Whatever this is, let's get to it."

Her gaze shifted away. She stood. Monks released her, waiting to see if she would walk out.

"I could use a cigarette," she said. She called to the bartender, "Warren, another one, please. I'll be right back." He was washing glasses and did not look up.

Monks followed her out onto Clement Street,

moderately busy with late-night traffic. Alison paused to search in her purse. Monks noted that she was still smoking Marlboro Lights, and still wearing a single ring, an elliptical black opal, on her right hand. Bachelor's degree from Radcliffe, psychology doctorate from Stanford, post-doc work at UCSF. The kind of facial bone structure that spoke of generations of blue blood, and plenty of money. Chapley, she had once told him, was from DeChaplais, Huguenots who had come to this country fleeing persecution in the early eighteenth century, and had kept track of every ancestor before and since.

It was a package she could have parlayed into anything she wanted. What she had chosen was to specialize in the treatment of dangerously violent men.

"I quit smoking for two years," she murmured, cigarette in mouth.

Monks was not one to criticize a self-destructive vice. He took her lighter and watched her hair spill forward, brushing her neck as she leaned into the flame.

He said, "I'm flattered that you remembered me, Alison. I'm waiting to find out why."

She exhaled, a thin stream of smoke that blended with the fog.

"Still in the investigation business?"

"Strictly armchair," Monks said warily. "Same as always."

"Someone's been coming around to people I know, asking questions about me. He's posing as a state licensing inspector. Says he's checking me out for a job, and I haven't applied for any."

"What kind of questions?"

"Partying. That sort of thing."

"Did your friends get his name?"

"Stryker. And I didn't say they were my friends."

Monks said, "People you bought drugs from?"

She nodded curtly. "One. Who's seriously annoyed at me right now. He thinks I shot my mouth off and that Stryker's an undercover cop."

"I assume this didn't come out of the blue."

She started walking again. Monks paced beside her.

"You know the term NGI?" she said.

He did. *Not Guilty by reason of Insanity*, the designation for psychotically violent offenders who were found unable to understand the criminal nature of their act. In California, they were outside the criminal justice system and not subject to regular imprisonment. Usually they were remanded to high-security mental institutions.

"I've been consulting for Clevinger Hospital, in the East Bay," she said. "It has a top-line NGI rehabilitation program. Big-time funding and prestige."

Monks knew about Clevinger, a county institution with a psych ward that verged on the notorious: by all accounts a cheerless place.

He said, "The money must be good."

"With the county? You know damned well it's not."

"Then what's the draw?"

"A chance to work with the great man who founded the program. At least that's what I thought."

"Who's the man?"

"A psychiatrist named Francis Jephson. He's British. Heard of him?"

Monks shook his head. "I don't deal much with psychiatrists."

"He was very polite all through the hiring process, but it didn't take me long to figure out he didn't want anything to do with me," she said. "He conducts all the NGI therapy in private. All their testing. When I offered to help, he patted me on the hand and told me in so many words to go powder my nose."

Monks's laugh was involuntary. "Sorry. He obviously doesn't know you very well."

"It pissed me off." She ground out the cigarette against a lamppost.

Monks waited.

"One of the NGIs is scheduled for release next month," she said. "John James Garlick. He's a woman beater: hospitalized several girlfriends, finally killed one."

"He's getting out?"

"Officially, he's been a model rehab client."

"Just asking."

"I don't like it either. I've been having problems with him from the first. I've caught him baiting the general ward patients in calculating ways."

"That's a red flag?"

"One of several. Signs that there's no real thought disorder. So I took a good hard look at his file. Everything was nice and neat. Too neat, especially this."

She took a manila envelope from her purse and pulled out several sheets of paper. She held one up to the lit front of a shop. Monks could make out a graph with perhaps a dozen lines plotted across.

"It's called the Psychosis Assessment Profile," she said. "It's administered every few months to rate patient improvement and adjust medications. One of the tests I'm supposed to give that Jephson won't let me. Garlick's shows him going from highly psychotic to within the normal range, over twenty-two months. I've been a clinician twelve years now, Rasp, and I know what I see. Garlick is no more psychotic than you or I. He never was."

Monks said, "The graph's a fake?"

"That's just openers. I started thinking I'd seen a file like that before. It took me a while to remember: a man who was released right after I started at Clevinger: Caymas Schulte. He'd raped and strangled a nine-year-old boy. I wasn't around him much, but I had the same take as with

John Garlick: dangerous, sociopathic, but in control of his actions. I went into the records library one night after the regular staff was gone. Went through ten years of files and found Caymas Schulte's, and three more besides."

She held up the remaining sheets of paper, fanned out to show the graphed lines. Except for minor variations, they were identical.

"All with similar diagnoses, schizo-affective disorders," she said. "All reporting similar reactions in the same categories. The same steady improvement. There are probably others I missed. I think they're sociopaths that Jephson's been selecting. Not every patient: maybe one in eight or ten. He provides them a false diagnosis of schizophrenia, then coaches them through his program."

She folded her arms, as if daring him to disagree.

"I believe you, Alison," Monks said. "But I don't get the why of it."

"It gives him a statistical edge that keeps him top dog. They're guaranteed successes."

Monks had seen his share of medical scams, but usually the payoff was obvious: cash.

He said, "You think he's embezzling from his funding?"

"I don't think it's about money. You're talking an ego that's off the charts. He was a *wunderkind* thirty years ago. Cambridge, Princeton. But he made claims he couldn't back up. He kept changing jobs—moving down the ladder. A place like Clevinger's the end of the line. Or it was, until he started working his miracles."

"He's taking a hell of a risk."

"The real risk is to the public, Rasp. These men are out on the street after two years, with no parole and nobody keeping track of where they are. They're supposed to report to outpatient clinics for medications, but there's no way to make them. They can change areas, even identities, cover their tracks. They just don't have any conscience, and there's no therapy for that. Like John Garlick. He'll be out in a few weeks and he's going to kill more women, I know it."

Monks stepped away, clasping his hands behind his back. The night wind brought the scent of wet salt air, and with it came a touch of memory: standing on the bridge of a navy troop transport, starting west across the Pacific from Mare Island.

He said, "Did you confront Jephson?"

"I tried to spook him. I told him I'd found out that some of the released NGIs had stopped reporting for meds and named the men with the phony charts. He sat there like an iceberg: that fucking British reserve. He knows damned well that if I take him on, I'm the one who's going to get hammered."

Monks smiled grimly. "Whistle-blowers tend to lose friends." It was a lesson he had learned the hard way.

"It finally started sinking in that was why he

approved my appointment. I was just what he wanted: junior, female, dumb."

Her eyes were wet and angry. Monks's hand moved to touch her cheek, a gesture so instinctive it surprised him. He stopped himself, letting his hand fall back to his side.

"Dumb enough to find out something nobody else suspects?" he said.

"Dumb enough to shoot my mouth off and warn him. I'll bet you anything that man Stryker, the one asking the questions about me, is a private detective. Jephson's trying to find something to fire me. I'm good at my job, dammit. It's nobody's business what I do in my own time."

A lot of people wouldn't agree, Monks thought. Starting with the SFPD and the American Psychological Association.

He said, "What makes me worth an antique razor?"

She smiled, brushing her eyes with the back of her hand.

"I want you to slice open Jephson's rotten spot."

"Rotten spot?"

"You know the name Vandenard?"

He blinked. "I've seen it in the society pages. I don't travel much in that part of the newspaper."

She held up the manila envelope again.

"I've been doing my homework. Robert Vandenard, the family's main heir, murdered a man back in '84."

A vague recollection of the event tugged at Monks's memory.

"He committed suicide later, didn't he?" Monks said. "The Vandenard boy?"

"There was a lot that happened in between that wasn't made public. Jephson got him pronounced NGI. Not long after that, the Clevinger program got funded big-time."

Monks said, "Let me guess. By Vandenard Foundation money."

"No surprise, huh?"

"That sort of thing happens all the time," Monks said. "I could see it as questionable ethics. But not illegal."

"How about what came next? Robby Vandenard was one of Jephson's first admissions. Instead of life in Atascadero, he did twenty-four easy months in Clevinger, and he was out, free as a bird."

Monks's gaze turned east, to the misted lights of the grand hotels on Nob Hill: the Mark Hopkins, the Sir Francis Drake, the Fairmont, holding themselves like wealthy dowagers in dated finery, looking coldly down on the upstart newer buildings of the city.

The kind of money where the line between illegality and questionable ethics could be erased.

"I need to find something on Jephson to protect myself, Rasp," she said. "I don't like fighting dirty. But I don't have any choice."

"Blackmail isn't in my line, Alison."

"I'm not talking blackmail. I'm talking about taking down a bad physician, outside the courtroom. Isn't that what you do?"

She was watching him. Her hair and skin wore a faint damp sheen of mist. Monks tried to sort through his emotions. The evening's events in the Emergency Room, still playing in his mind like a background tape. The invisible chain of responsibility tugging him to return to the hospital. His past with Alison Chapley, with that uneasiness still close to the surface.

Her nearness, now, this minute.

Monks said, "I'll think it over. I'd better get back."

She handed him the sheaf of papers.

"Can you come back inside for just a minute? There's someone I'd like you to talk to."

Her wineglass had not been refilled. The bartender was at the far end talking to friends, and ignored her signal for what seemed to Monks a pointedly long time. Finally he approached with obvious coolness, a stocky man with a handlebar mustache and a tilt to his head.

"Warren, this is Dr. Monks." Neither offered a hand. "He's an investigator," she said. "He's going to help me about that man who said he was from the licensing board. Will you tell him what you told me?"

The bartender shrugged. "It's history." He started moving away.

"Warren," she said. This time there was a faint tone of pleading. "It doesn't have anything to do with here, it's somebody trying to get me fired from my job. I'm *going* to get it straight."

He leaned forward across the bar and said with sudden harsh intensity, "Are you fucking crazy? First that and now this?" His head gestured contemptuously at Monks. "There's a million bars in this town, honey. Go find one."

Sudden comprehension came to Monks. The bartender was her drug connection, a not-friend who assumed that Alison had drawn the attention of police. He had cut her off, and that was why she had brought Monks here: to repair the damage.

He knew how it went: irritations and tension building into anger that hovered just below the surface, until finally something, usually something small, pushed the button and you blew up, usually at the wrong person.

Usually, you did not care.

Monks said to him, "Where'd you get the cowboy hat?"

His eyes narrowed. "I don't own a cowboy hat."

"I can see it."

The bartender reared back, then thrust a finger toward Monks's chest. "You're *out* of here, asshole."

"I've got a special dictionary at home," Monks said. "Next to the word 'shitweasel,' there's a picture looks just like you."

He walked to the door, half expecting the bartender to follow, his mind already supplying novelty headlines for tomorrow's *Chronicle*: DOC DECKED IN DUKE-OUT, SAWBONES SLAMS SALOON STUD, PHYSICIAN FAILS TO HEAL SELF. The last time he had punched a man had been some years before, when he had taken a verbal cheap shot from a cardiac surgeon in a hospital cafeteria line, but you could not really call that a fight.

He waited on the sidewalk, fists tightening when the door opened. It was Alison, alone.

"I'm sorry," she said. "I had no idea."

Monks said, "Yeah, you did."

She smiled, very slightly, the look of a child found out in something mischievous.

"You can take the boy out of Chicago, but you can't take Chicago out of the boy."

He shook his head and walked on, but allowed himself to be caught, his arm hugged, a warm wet kiss planted on his cheek.

"Are we still on?" she said.

He nodded stiffly.

They paused at her car. Monks recognized it with confused warmth: a vintage champagne-colored Mercedes sedan that had been the scene of more than one fevered teen-style coupling.

He held the door open. She brushed deliberately against him as she slid behind the wheel.

"You left just when things were starting to get interesting," she said.

Monks watched her go, back to the Bolinas

house with its windows that turned golden in the afternoon sun and its ocean-facing deck where she had first begun to unveil herself to him.

Alison Chapley might not like fighting dirty, but she surely knew how.

Monks got back to the hospital a little before midnight. Fatigue had settled on him, and he had decided on a nap before taking on charts. In the old days, thirty-six hours on his feet had been routine, but now half that was pushing it. He walked to the ER physicians' office, a room just big enough to hold a desk, sink, and cot, and unlocked the door quietly, not wanting to wake another doc who might have beat him to it.

The interior was dim, and it took him perhaps three seconds to absorb the tiny bytes of visual information. There was a figure on the cot, but not sleeping: sitting upright. A man with a youngish face topped by straw-colored hair. He stared back at Monks, mouth open in dismay.

Vernon Dickhaut.

A second figure, wearing the top half of an ER nurse's magenta uniform, was crouched between his splayed legs, fingers positioned as if gripping a clarinet. Her head swiveled, eyes flaring like those of a deer caught in headlights. There was a faint wet popping sound and a glimpse of glistening pink flesh.

Monks coughed. "Excuse me. I just need to grab this." He scooped his daypack from the

desk, keeping his back turned to the frozen figures, and closed the door quietly behind him.

Nothing like crisis to bring out that life-
affirming instinct, he thought, and trudged out to
the Bronco to try to catch some sleep.

•

3

The next morning, Monks sat in the physicians' office washing down ibuprofen with night-old coffee and dictating charts in standardized medical format.

ESPOSITO, ISMAEL

CHIEF COMPLAINT
Multiple gunshot wounds to chest and abdomen.

HISTORY OF PRESENT ILLNESS
Mr. Esposito is in his mid teens—

Monks's mouth twitched at the use of present tense, but this was catch-up work, theoretically done before the outcome was known.

—with no history in this hospital. Approximately 30 minutes before admission, he was wounded in a street gunfight.

The desk phone rang.

"Carroll! What the fuck are we, Mother Teresa? Surgery alone is going to be five thousand bucks!"

The voice was a familiar one, blending elements of growl and shout: Baird Necker, the hospital's chief financial officer, who presumably had just arrived and found the incident report on his desk. As expected, neither of the gunshot casualties had either cash or insurance. There would be minimal compensation from the city and possibly bits from MediCal. Not nearly enough to cover the costs.

"I think everybody involved was aware that this wasn't a money-making situation," Monks said. "You know, the people who were up to their elbows in mesentery?"

A pause. Monks waited patiently. Baird looked and behaved something like a boxer dog, a fierce-presenting alpha male, but he could never last long without lapsing into fundamental decency.

More sedately, he said, "I understand our obligation, Carroll. But we've got to find a way to control this kind of thing. It'll drive us under."

"They're not going to stop shooting each other, Baird. They seem to like it."

"We can't help anybody if we're out of business, right?" A wheedling tone had crept in.

"Next time Triage Base calls, *you* tell them no."

A longer pause, and at last, a heavy exhalation. "Okay, I'll try to split the damage up so everybody gets fucked equally."

The phone slammed down, then rang again instantly. "Sorry about the kid," Baird said, and hung up.

Monks gave a final glance at the chart of Ismael Esposito, then stood and poured another half cup from the urn. It gave off a burnt smell. Ismael had lasted less than an hour. When the surgeons went in, they found two finger-sized holes in the abdominal aorta, a situation that allowed them approximately one minute after deflation of the MAST suit before the heart emptied of blood. They managed to clamp the aorta in time, but could not have known that the right pulmonary artery had also been clipped and weakened by the lung-puncturing bullet. The renewed pressure from the clamped aorta blew it open. By the time they got into his chest, his system had pumped the right lung full of blood, and they were simply unable to catch up again. The technical term was *exsanguination*.

Rafael Vasquez had been transferred to the medical facility of SF County jail, and Ismael's brother, finally quieted by reality, had been taken in for questioning. The flattened slugs would make their way from pathology to some ballistics warehouse, there to remain, in the unlikely event they might ever be matched to weapons.

It was a few minutes after 8 A.M. Monks was not due back for five more days, one of the benefits of emergency medicine: he preferred working two or three shifts at short intervals, then taking several days to himself. He had been planning a favorite excursion: a long, lazy canoe drift on Tomales Bay, with a cooler of sandwiches—hard salami, roast beef, Swiss cheese, and kraut, dripping with vinegar dressing—washed down with bottles of icy Moretti beer.

He stacked the charts and turned to the papers that Alison Chapley had given him.

On top were the five Psychosis Assessment Profiles she had shown him: John James Garlick, still in Clevinger, and four other NGIs who had been released over the past several years. Each sheet had a graph of the test's results, ratings from one to one hundred in a dozen categories: hallucinations, voices, self-control, anger, paranoia, and so on. The lines on each graph were dated, showing the test's results at roughly three-month intervals. All five showed significant improvement within the two-year rehabilitation period, from highly psychotic to acceptably normal.

Monks superimposed the graphs onto each other, one at a time. There were minor variations, occasional jumps or lapses, slightly different numerical ratings, but the overall similarity was clear.

On each sheet, Alison had jotted a brief history of the patient.

Prokuta, Wayne. Heavy drug user, supporting this with robberies of increasing violence. Finally beat to death an elderly woman with her iron. Diagnosed with schizo-affective disorder, dual problems of schizophrenia and bipolarity. Admitted 7/9/88. Released 8/3/90, to parents' home in Sacramento. Aged 27 at the time of release.

Foote, Kenneth. A biker with a history of sudden savage assaults. Facing a second manslaughter charge and life in prison for stabbing a college student who sat on his Harley. Diagnosed paranoid schizophrenic, with a chemical imbalance in the brain, correctable by medications. Admitted 10/12/90. Released 12/18/92, to an apartment in San Jose. Aged 38.

Kurlin, Brad. History of childhood antisocial behavior triad. Terrorized his wealthy adoptive parents through his teens. Living in a San Francisco apartment they provided him, set a fire in a transient hotel that claimed six lives. Diagnosed with schizo-affective disorder. Admitted 4/14/93. Released 2/21/95, to parents in Mill Valley. Aged 23.

Schulte, Caymas. Known molester of several children, finally murdered nine-year-old boy. Intimately familiar with the Mendocino backwoods. Savage assault on a search party member who had tracked him there. Diagnosed paranoid schizophrenic. Admitted 11/6/94. Released 10/3/96, to mother's home in Mendocino. Aged 34.

At the bottom of each account, a final note: *No longer reporting as required to outpatient clinics for medications. Present whereabouts unknown.*

Monks turned to the remaining papers: a dozen photocopied newspaper clippings, most of them chronicling an event from the late summer of 1984. A man named Merle Lutey had been shot dead by Robert Vandenard IV, the only son of a prominent San Francisco family. Lutey was a hired hand on the Vandenards' estate in the wine country of Napa.

The first, longer, articles noted that the family was marked by tragedy. A teenaged daughter, Katherine, had been murdered by a transient years earlier. Robert IV, known as Robby, had a history of mental illness, including paranoid delusions. A blurred photo showed a thin-faced man in handcuffs being led away by sheriffs. He looked to be in his twenties, but the photographer had caught something old and knowing in the eyes.

Monks noted that the story went from front page headlines in the *San Francisco Chronicle* to a small paragraph in the back pages within a week. There were no later reports about the murder: no mention of the NGI ruling, or of Robby

Vandenard's admission to Jephson's program.

But Robby created another small stir when he went missing in late 1988. He was found the following spring, in the woods near the same Napa estate, dead of a self-inflicted gunshot wound.

There was one final short clip, dated August 18, 1971, presumably printed as a curiosity item.

> *PSYCHIATRIST SNAKEBIT*
> *Santa Rosa (AP)—*
> *Dr. Francis Jephson, a resident psychiatrist at Letterman Hospital in San Francisco, was bitten by a rattlesnake while hiking near Calistoga yesterday.*
>
> *Jephson was treated at Santa Rosa Memorial Hospital and released. The attending physician, Dr. Richard Merriman, said the hospital typically saw two or three cases of snakebite per year. They are rarely fatal except in unusual circumstances, but should be taken seriously and treated promptly, Merriman said.*

Monks put his elbows on the desk, closed his eyes, and pressed his fingertips against his temples. Francis Jephson, from Cambridge and Princeton: stellar beginnings that had slid down into compromise, and then, if Alison was right, ethics violations that might be criminal.

A man who was snakebit.

I'm talking about taking down a bad physician, outside the courtroom. Isn't that what you do?

In fact, it was.

Then there was the other aspect, unspoken but close to the surface. That whatever lovers she might have encountered in the intervening years were gone. That she seemed willing to give it another try.

As for him, it was not as if he had much to lose.

The sound of a key turning in the door brought Monks up startled. Vernon Dickhaut stepped in, saw him, and retreated, mumbling, "Sorry, Doc."

"No, no, come on in," Monks said.

"I'm on shift again this afternoon," Vernon said. "I thought maybe I'd catch a couple of hours sleep."

Monks remembered all too well the life of a resident, with hundred-plus-hour weeks at the hospital.

"By all means. I was just leaving." He stood, stuffing the papers into his daypack.

Vernon hovered, looking sheepish. "Uh, last night. I realize that was out of line."

"You may regret some of the ones you do, Vernon," Monks said kindly, "but believe me, you'll regret all the ones you don't."

In the lobby, Monks paused at a phone kiosk and spent a moment considering. The obvious person to bring in on this was Stover Larrabee, a private detective who did most of the investigative legwork for the malpractice insurance group,

ASCLEP. Larrabee did not keep regular hours, and it was always a crap shoot as to when to reach him.

The phone, an unlisted and very private home number, rang nine times before a sleepy and displeased woman picked up. Monks tried to remember the name of Larrabee's last girlfriend, but could not—that was another gamble anyway.

He introduced himself, and added, "Sorry to call so early."

The apology did not seem to impress her. There came a slapping sound, as of the phone hitting flesh, and her muttered words, "Something about a monk."

Larrabee's tone was vaguely defensive. "I should have checked in with you, Carroll. I think we've got DeMers right where we want him." The reference was to an ASCLEP case coming up tomorrow.

"I didn't call to criticize, Stover."

"It's been tricky. You wouldn't want to talk either, if you'd paid a hundred grand to beat somebody out of a kidney."

"A hundred grand? I might just look into retraining."

"Think it over. There's going to be a vacancy real soon."

"I need some advice," Monks said. "An unrelated matter."

"I'm a more caring person after morning."

"How about lunch? On me, of course."

"Club Trieste, Columbus near Broadway," Larrabee said promptly.

"Noon?"

"Let's make it one."

Monks said, "Do you know a private investigator named Stryker?"

"Not off hand." Larrabee sounded annoyed. "I thought I knew everybody working around here. Did you get a description?"

"Maybe forty, tough-looking. He's posing as a mental health licensing inspector."

"It sounds like the kind of phony name some swinging dick would dream up," Larrabee said. "I'll see what I can find out."

Monks stopped in the locker room to wash and shave. For the first time in months, he paused to study his appearance. He had inherited his mother's black Irish coloring, which his ex-wife had attributed to the long-ago pity of some lonely colleen for a shipwrecked armada sailor: hair dark and wiry, going grizzled but still mostly there; eyes green with the whites faintly muddy, staring out with an intensity that verged on anger. Face networked with old acne scars and lined with deepening creases like ravines splitting the earth. Arched nose that had thickened and teeth that needed work. Bushy, wild eyebrows that had earned him his mad monk nickname. He was reasonably conscientious about exercise, but had been letting it slide of late, and could feel the softening of his chest, the rounding of his shoulders. He vowed, without enthusiasm, to improve.

His feelings were awry, and it took him a moment to identify the cause. It was not quite happiness, but something more or perhaps less, like a wary satisfaction at rejoining a battle after standing on the sidelines for years.

4

Monks drove into North Beach a few minutes before 1 p.m. and found a parking place on Kearney Street, an event so unusual he could only attribute it to an attentive parking angel, or perhaps the weather. On Columbus a hard steady wind blew in from the Pacific, and he walked against it with head down and hands in pockets. The topless joints like Big Al's and the Condor were still going strong, but over the last twenty-odd years, the emphasis had gone to full nudity and then to live sex. He threaded his way through leering bouncers trying to hook him in, and continued on until he found Club Trieste. Standing on the sidewalk, he could hear the throb of music from inside. So this was Larrabee's idea of lunch. Given the neighborhood, the advertisements were, he supposed, comparatively tasteful. He stepped inside.

The room was dark except for a reddish-lit stage at the far end. He could feel the music's baseline through his shoes. "Cover's ten bucks," a voice said.

Monks blinked, trying to find its owner, whom he judged to be a not very friendly woman. "Pay or beat it," she said, the tone harder still. He began to perceive her outline, standing in front of him: thin, shorter than his level of vision, dark-haired, and wearing a long black cocktail dress, a sort of waifish Morticia Addams look. This, he reasoned, would be the hostess. Behind her, a very large man in a dark shirt was starting to move toward him. Monks extracted a ten from his wallet, trying not to look rushed.

"That buys you the first one," she said. Visions of vodka flashed through his mind, but it was still too early.

"Club soda. Rocks. Lemon. I'm supposed to meet a friend."

"Take your pick," she said, and moved aside. The large man receded. Monks's eyes were adjusting. The place was what he had heard described as a splash palace: black Naugahyde, red trim and chrome, music like noisy velour. A bar ran along one wall, with the rest of the room taken by tables. About half were occupied by one or more men. It could have been a Holiday Inn, except for the lighting, cocktail waitresses wear-

ing only V-shaped thongs, and the stares fixed on
the stage, where a pretty Asian girl was performing a routine that centered around a firepole,
with occasional forays onto the runway. Monks
gathered from what remained of her outfit, a G-
string roughly the size of a locket, that she was
near the end of her set.

"She hasn't quite got that kick down yet,"
Larrabee said, at his elbow. Monks followed him
to a table at the far end from the stage, an area
uncrowded and comparatively quiet.

Larrabee was a burly man with a roosterlike
shock of dark hair. He was wearing a rumpled
corduroy sport coat and a hand-painted silk tie
that featured a pheasant bursting from cover. He
had grown up in Flint, Michigan, his father a
Tennessee mountain boy who had migrated
north to work in the auto plants. This upbringing
had resulted in a hybrid mode of speech—a flat
Midwest accent, punctuated by hillbilly drawl
and tempered by California usage—which had an
unsettling way of not quite melding. He had
spent twelve years on the SFPD before going private, and was good at getting people to tell things
they did not want known. He was drinking
Heineken from a bottle. He preferred Pabst in a
can, but presumably it was not available here.

Monks's ten-dollar club soda arrived just as the
dancer teased her way out of the G-string, revealing a pubis barbered to a small black arrowhead
diving south. As the music ended, men tossed

bills onto the stage, which she gathered up along with her costume before prancing into the wings.

"Is that your friend?" Monks said.

"She's coming two, three down the line. You see anything you like, I could look into it. Some of them are owned."

"I'll let it go for now."

A voice came over the sound system, more than slightly reminiscent of Wolfman Jack, introducing the next dancer: Lucinda. Monks realized there was a disc jockey in a booth at the stage's far end. It was an oddly personal touch. He had assumed the music was all taped.

Larrabee said, "I couldn't find any other licensed investigator in the Bay Area named Stryker. He might be from out of town. He might be bullshit. What's he after?"

Monks told him.

"Alison operates like she can't be touched," he finished. "Then something catches up with her, and she's outraged. Maybe it's the way she grew up."

"Anything like this happen before?"

"I went with her once to buy back some photos she'd let a guy take of her. Nasty little situation."

Larrabee spent a moment pushing his beer back and forth between his forefingers, then drained it. He craned around to catch the waitress's attention, making a circling motion over their drinks.

"If she wants to reopen the Robby Vandenard

case, she's got a big job," Larrabee said. "It was a long time ago. People forget, move, die. Anybody who was involved officially isn't about to admit that anything hinky went on. And let's face it: she'd come under the microscope."

"That's exactly what she doesn't want. Just something she can use to make Jephson back off."

"In that case, I'd say: *cherchez le hard-on*."

"Meaning?"

"Look for somebody who feels ripped off, starting with the family of the guy Robby Vandenard killed. Robbie walked, and your man Jephson engineered it."

"Are you for hire?"

Larrabee nodded.

"Let's go pay a call on the widow."

Their drinks arrived. The waitress looked older than the dancers: heavily made-up, friendly, but in a way that seemed worn. Monks wondered how many hands she had fended off through how many years.

Larrabee's gaze shifted suddenly. Monks turned to see a young woman walking toward them, wearing a satin teal hip-length wrap and three-inch heels of matching color. She was in her late twenties and very pretty, with auburn hair tumbling halfway down her back, the long slender legs of a swimsuit model, and the slightly hard look of a girl who had thought things were going to turn out differently. She sat beside

Larrabee, her hand moving to his thigh. He introduced her as Debbie. Monks started to say, *I think we spoke on the phone*, but caught himself in time. It might not have been her.

"Stover told me you're a doctor," she said. She leaned forward, parting the wrap. "I just had these done. You mind telling me what you think?"

He started to point out that plastic surgery was not his specialty, but by then she had unhooked the front of her halter, also teal, of a decorative scallop design. She inhaled slowly. Her breasts rose with her exquisite rib cage. She cupped and hefted them. When she let go, they bounced, once.

"Very professional, in my estimation," Monks said, sitting back and folding his arms. "A symmetry not often met with."

"I hope so," she said, hooking up again. "They cost me three thousand bucks apiece and a month off work." She stood and kissed Larrabee's cheek. "I'm up next."

Sadly, Monks watched her hurry off.

He said, "I don't mean to pry, but wasn't there a grad student doing her thesis on you?"

"They come and they go, Doc. Soon as this is over, I'll see if I can find an address. What was the name?"

"Lutey. Merle."

Larrabee grinned.

"That's got Okie written all over it."

Debbie advanced onto the stage, the disc jockey announcing her as Secret. In that light, she looked younger. The two men watched in a respectful silence shared by the rest of the audience while the six thousand dollars worth of remodeled tissue was musically unveiled.

That was the way it was, Monks thought. You went more than a year without a taste, and just when you thought you were over the whole thing, the world conspired to throw it in your face every time you turned around.

Larrabee said, "Mrs. Lutey—"

"Not anymore."

Larrabee passed his hand over his shock of hair, embarrassed. Boyish. Disarming.

"Awfully sorry. My information's old." He opened his wallet and showed his PI license.

The former Mrs. Lutey stood in her doorway with her arms folded and her jaw set in a way that suggested that she was used to dealing with authorities. She was not much over thirty, which put her still in her teens at the time of her husband's death: strawberry blond, wearing skin tight jeans that accentuated her almost anorexic thinness, and a long-sleeved sweatshirt.

"We've been hired by someone who's interested in the case of Robert Vandenard and your, uh, late husband," Larrabee said. "We wonder if you'd take a minute to discuss this with us."

"Who's the someone?"

"A psychologist, a lady like yourself. She's uncovered some irregularities, and now she feels her career's being threatened. Look, Mrs.—"

"My name's Darla."

"Darla, please call me Stover, and this is my associate, Dr. Monks."

Monks murmured a greeting and stayed in the background.

They were in the outskirts of Boyes Springs, a northern extension of Sonoma known for its drug subculture and population of ex-cons. The house was old, small, with checked clapboard siding and blistered paint. The yard suggested kids of all ages. A swing set and other toys were scattered around, along with several trikes, bicycles, and a Bondo-gray TransAm with the hood off.

"We know that must have been a very difficult time for you," Larrabee said, "especially being up against a family so powerful, like the Vandenards. Did you—if you don't mind my asking very frankly—did you feel you were treated with fairness? I mean, obviously you were deeply injured, losing your husband."

"Are you going to open the case back up?"

"That could depend heavily on your cooperation, Darla."

She looked from one to the other of them, making up her mind about something. It was a kind of look Monks had seen before, and abruptly he realized where: in the ER, junkies faking pain to con him for a shot of narcotics.

She said, "I'd go for it."

"Can you tell us what happened between your husband and Robby Vandenard?"

She shrugged, her thin shoulders piercing the sweatshirt with skeletal outlines.

"Nobody saw the shooting, but probably the only person surprised was Merle."

"Why do you say that?"

Music started suddenly inside the house, blaring metallic rock. She ignored it. "Merle was a bully. He pushed around anybody he figured he could."

"Including you?"

"He'd get drunk and beat the shit out of me."

"Is that why you didn't press the case?"

She leaned back inside and yelled, "Turn that down, goddamn it!" A door slammed, reducing the volume.

She closed the front door and leaned wearily back against it.

"Why didn't I press the case? There were two lawyers here even before the police. That's how I got the news that Merle was dead. They were like uncles at a funeral, pretending they gave a shit. They left me a thousand dollars cash. Told me that would help me through the next couple days, and they'd be back to talk."

Larrabee said, "Vandenard lawyers?"

She nodded.

"And they came back with an offer to compensate you?"

"Fifty thousand. It was either that or spend a lot of money I didn't have, that wouldn't have done any good anyway. I put up with Merle more than five years. I deserved to get something."

"Did anybody else know about this?"

"Nobody that counted. They made me sign a bunch of papers, told me I was giving up my right to sue. I don't know if it was true or not. I didn't care, then."

"Why would you be willing to come forward now?"

"I called him to ask for a loan, a couple years ago. The motherfucker wouldn't even talk to me."

"You mean the attorney?"

"Yeah. Capaldi."

"Bernard Capaldi?"

"That's him."

Larrabee's mouth twitched. Monks had heard the name, too. Bernard Capaldi was the kind of old-time lawyer whose strings went inestimably deep into politics, property, and possibly, crime: the major affairs of the city.

She said, "When I got that check, I thought it was going to last forever."

Monks was willing to bet that most of that fifty thousand dollars had gone up her nose, or arm, or both.

"Darla," he said, "did you ever meet Robby Vandenard?"

"A few times."

"You think the insanity defense was a lie?"

"He was crazy, all right. But not the kind of crazy where he didn't know what he was doing; the kind where he just did whatever he wanted. Creepy. Everybody was scared of him."

"What kind of things did he do that scared people?"

"Besides killing his sister?"

Monks realized that his mouth had opened. He closed it.

Larrabee said, "Would you say that again?"

"It got blamed on somebody else. But that's what the old-timers around the place thought."

"When did that happen?"

"When he was a kid, eleven or twelve."

"Jesus wept." Larrabee stepped away, hands going into his pockets.

"You guys didn't know about that?"

"We knew she'd been murdered," Monks said. "Not that Robby was suspected. Did that information come up in the case?"

The bony shrug again. "I wasn't invited to the hearing. But I know that's how it got turned around. They said Robby was paranoid, that he thought Merle was the guy who'd killed Katherine, coming back for him. What bullshit."

"Darla." Larrabee passed his hand over his hair. "You say that Merle pushed around people he figured he could. Why would he take on somebody scary like Robby?"

The appraising stare came into her eyes again,

judging whether giving away more information was going to buy her anything.

"Merle was a good-looking guy," she finally said. "He'd done a couple years in Santa Rita."

Larrabee said, "Are you saying he and Robby had a sexual relationship?"

"Merle thought he was going to get money out of Robby." She smiled suddenly. It made her look almost pretty.

"Guess he was right," she said.

5

Alison Chapley parked in the staff lot of Clevinger Hospital and lit one more cigarette. She stayed in her car, watching Psychiatric Unit Number Three, known as Three-Psych.

This was a flat I-shaped building at the center of the hospital's grounds. It had an asphalt courtyard surrounded by a twelve-foot-high cyclone fence, topped with turned-in iron spikes and strung with razor-wire. In the corners, video cameras perched like vultures on high stalks. There was a single basketball hoop with no net, and a worn heavy punching bag hung on a welded chain.

Several men were standing inside the fence smoking or pacing, or talking to each other or to no one visible. Even from that distance, there was something unsettling about the way they moved.

These were the NGIs: at any given time, eight to ten men on-ward who had killed or seriously injured others, had been found by the courts Not Guilty by reason of Insanity and been recommended for psychiatric treatment instead of regular prison. The program here was known as JCOG: the Jephson Cognitive Therapy for Management of Psychotically Violent Behavior at Clevinger Memorial Hospital.

Almost all the JCOG inmates had lengthy records, with several stays in prisons or institutions before new psychiatric evaluations triggered the NGI ruling. Roughly eleven percent washed out within the first weeks. Most of the rest achieved stability, enforced by combinations of Haldol, Ativan, Clozapine, and lithium, with an average stay of twenty-two months, then were released as rehabilitated.

From her car, Alison could identify most of them: Perez, Holger, Odum—aggravated assault, child abuse, manslaughter. The fourth NGI was a good-looking man with dark spiky hair, wearing gray hospital pajamas: John James Garlick, soon to be released. Garlick was standing well apart from the others, talking to someone his body was blocking. She could not see who it was.

She got out of the car and started up the walk. Except for Three-Psych's razor-wire fence and a patrolling security car, the hospital could have been an aging junior college: three acres of grassy hillside with half a dozen unattractive, functional buildings surrounding the original brick structure. The afternoon was heavy with clouds, but flashes of sunlight brightened the old brick. She wondered what the philanthropist founder, turn-of-the-century *grande dame* Edith Clevinger, would think of her pretty hospital now.

Alison unlocked the main door to Three-Psych and walked down the hall to the courtyard's inside entrance, stopping in the doorway.

By chance or instinct, Garlick swiveled with feral speed. His eyes were already focused when they met hers, hard as a stag beetle's shell, seeming able to pierce her thoughts and perhaps her very being. Two seconds later his gaze moved on as if the contact had never happened, leaving a faint chill, as if something had been taken away.

The man he was talking to stepped aside, a hasty move that had a guilty appearance. She could see who it was now.

Dr. Francis Jephson.

Jephson said something more to Garlick, then crossed the courtyard to where she stood. He wore an expensive gray wool suit, an ecru shirt with cufflinks, and gold-rimmed glasses over pale blue eyes.

"Alison. Could you wander by my office in a few minutes?"

"Of course, Doctor."

"We do need to talk." It seemed to her that he emphasized the word *do* ominously.

She nodded and watched him leave: slim, balanced, moving with an athletic stride. He had been a distance runner at Cambridge and still trained with exacting discipline.

Garlick had moved to the courtyard's far end, a lone figure staring out through the fence at the freedom which, in a few weeks, would be his.

Garlick, who had arrived twenty months earlier from the maximum security facility at Atascadero, along with a detailed report on the incident that had landed him there: gripping his girlfriend by the hair and repeatedly ramming her face into a bathroom sink until a sliver of skull pierced her brain.

Who had assaulted two ex-wives and several other girlfriends in a similar way. Who tested significantly above normal in intelligence, with two years of college and a history of success as an electronics salesman. Who was ruled schizophrenic, but whose powers of persuasion had kept a string of women unwilling to testify against him.

Whose falsified psychiatric evaluation was her first inkling that Francis Jephson had been coaching a selected few.

Garlick, soon to be released.

Alison turned back inside and stopped short, almost running into a man passing by. He raised his hands apologetically and she smiled, but the thought flashed across her mind, as it had with Jephson, that he had moved too quickly, that she had caught him at something covert.

Perhaps, standing behind her, listening.

"Didn't mean to scare you, Dr. Chapley."

Harold Henley was the chief public service officer, a euphemism for guard. He stood six four and weighed close to three hundred pounds. He moved deliberately and spoke softly, and was the only person on the ward the NGIs feared as much as each other.

Abruptly, she wondered if he knew what Jephson had been doing, knew what she had found out. Harold had worked more than a decade at Clevinger, and not much in this small world escaped him.

"I'm a little jumpy today, Harold."

"Yeah?"

Rattled, she grasped for a diversion.

"I'm on the run from the law. I shot my boyfriend."

A flicker of respect showed in his eyes, as if she might lead a more interesting life than he had imagined.

"Fine example you set. You supposed to be showing these people how to act."

"He was insensitive. He treated me like an object and never did the dishes. There's not a court in the land would convict me."

Harold grinned fiercely. "Worse than that.

They'd sentence you to some kind of codependency group."

She walked on toward her office. He paced beside her, a thick fold of ebony skin bulging above his blue uniform collar as his head swiveled to scan the hall. His radio and nightstick hung like a child's toys on his massive hips.

Attendants and techs passed by on missions real or feigned. The hallway's interior colors gave the sense of having been put together out of leftovers from other buildings: the walls flat gray, the trim pink, the linoleum, heaved and uneven from decades of settling, a vague tan. The sharp smell of pine antiseptic cleaner blended with, but did not cover, the decades-old reek of urine and unwashed bodies. There were no handrails for the handicapped, for fear they would be torn off and used as weapons. Pastel floral prints, intended to be soothing, were immovably affixed. The kitchen had never contained a stove or sharp utensils.

She said, "You still want to sell that Buick?"

Harold's interest quickened. "You finally ready to get you a real car?"

"The Mercedes is a money sink," she admitted, "but I love it. Another bad relationship."

"Huh." He ruminated, then said, "Buick's gone. Ain't no money in cars."

"So what next?"

"Apartment building."

"An *apartment* building?"

He looked both embarrassed and proud. "You get in for next to nothing. Live there and manage till you own it. Then you buy another one."

"I never realized it was quite that easy." She unlocked her office door.

"You got to know some people. So next time you looking for an apartment, Alison, you tell Harold."

With others around, he was the essence of formality. But alone, he would call her by her first name, lapsing into street accent to shade the L into a W and drop the I. It was a sound personalized and gently possessive. Early on, perhaps the first moment she had walked on the ward, Harold had decided that here, in this place, she was his.

She smiled again. "You'll be my first call."

Her office door, like the others on the ward, locked itself behind her. She exhaled, annoyed at herself for her edginess.

But the sense was inescapable that she was the one locked in a cell. The room was tiny, packed with books, paperwork, and files. The desk she kept clear, a last outpost of defense against the surrounding chaos. Her gaze moved across a shelf of videotapes on assault management and AIDS protection; a medication list, a reminder that most psychiatric treatment came in the form of tranquilization; her teaching schedule, with the world *assault* figuring again and again. On the

ward, she wore earth-toned clothing, pale lipstick, and no jewelry or scarf that could be
grabbed.

She took out a compact, touched up her
makeup, and paused with her hand on the doorknob. She could hear more patients in the hall
now, word of her arrival having spread. Three-
Psych had been built to house thirty, which
meant in practice that the administration tried to
hold it down to fifty. Most of the non-NGIs were
public admissions from the community, compris-
ing the full spectrum of mental illness. They
gathered around her, and a part of her mind
believed that this was the best healing she could
give, just to be there.

She recognized most of the voices, not from
what they said or how, but a peculiar quality
beyond any of that, like vocal pheromones audi-
ble only to a tuned ear: Corinne, wrists and neck
heavily scarred, who occasionally stripped naked
and walked screaming down the hall; Lewis, who
could get drunk on water and had to be
restrained from bellying up to a toilet like a bar;
Edward, who had ripped antennas off cars in a
supermarket parking lot to keep them from
broadcasting his thoughts to the world, and who
now paced tensely, flipping the pages of a special
Bible to keep demons away. Many of the patients
reflected the vast range of subfrequencies known
as thought insertion, hearing the voices of angels,
demons, the dead, urging anything from suicide

to the sacrifice of a baby they pronounced evil; or sometimes voices just keeping them company. It was a major problem in maintaining schizophrenics on medications. Without those inner companions, they got lonesome.

When she stepped out of her office into the crowd that had gathered, some of the faces turned away with quick shyness, while other gazes clung like unseen nets, without social grace or remove, the straight blank curiosity of children or primitives.

"I need," a voice said. She turned to the man who stood shuffling in a slow dance of agitation: Raymond Coolidge, recently arrived from the streets of Oakland, late twenties, Psychosis Not Otherwise Specified, which in practice meant heroin addiction coupled with HIV dementia.

"Some *pussy*."

Raymond had the habit of declaring himself to whatever female staff or patients happened to be around when the urge struck him. His face was sweating and earnest, grayish skin stretched tight, leaning toward her at an odd angle as if his neck was broken. The thin fingers of his right hand ceaselessly moved up and down his thigh, squeezing his penis, which hung visibly inside his loose pajama pants.

"I need some pussy," he said again, more firmly now, as if she could not help but agree. "Now, baby. You got to understand." His flexing fingers left his thigh and hovered imploringly in the air between them. She considered the text-book response: explaining to this psychotic man, who stood before her massaging his cock, that his behavior was inappropriate.

"If you touch anybody, Raymond, you're going to Seclusion."

His face turned morose and he shuffled off, hand returning to its work. He was not known to be assaultive, but she decided to recommend increasing his Haldol dosage. Each four-person dorm slept eight, with patients close enough to touch each other and many unable to defend themselves or fully understand what might be happening.

The far end of the ward's I-shape was commanded by the Nurses' Station, which stood glassed-in like a gun turret on a raised dais. Past that were ten identical concrete cells, eight feet square, euphemistically called seclusion rooms. Furniture in each consisted of a one-piece stainless steel bed bolted to the floor. The windows in the steel doors were shock-resistant glass reinforced with wire mesh, too small for a human body to pass through if the glass were broken. Video cameras, recessed in the ceilings out of patient reach, broadcast twenty-four hours per day on a bank of monitors at the Nurses' Station.

Only the plastic-covered bedding was vulnerable to assault. The thin mattresses and pillows occasionally got shredded or eaten, but it was the sheets, provided for patient comfort by California law, that made the staff nervous. Before coming to Clevinger, Alison had not known that you could hang yourself—quickly—without your feet leaving the floor.

The Clevinger Administration Building was a different world from Three-Psych. Here the doors were not locked. Jephson's outer office was spacious, with the luxury of a large and ungrated window.

Paula Rivinius, Jephson's secretary, was on the phone. Mrs. R, as she was known on the wards, was dressed in a peacock-patterned sheath of lavender, purple, and cobalt. It was low-cut, slinky, laden with jewels, an outfit more at home at a Las Vegas dinner show featuring Tom Jones than in a hospital office. She was in her late forties, but worked hard to look ten years younger, and brought it off with fair success. Her longish hair was dark blond, the once black and now graying roots dyed and teased into careful disarray. Good legs and generous breasts allowed her to look Rubenesque rather than plump. Indigo eyeshadow and heavy jewelry lent an exotic, vaguely Eastern touch, as of a Hungarian gentlewoman in reduced circumstances.

She looked up over cat's-eye glasses and held up two fingers for minutes. From the conversation, it was clear that she was trying to place a patient in a halfway house. Alison walked to the window, her suspicions widening again to include

Mrs. R among those who might know about the phony NGIs. Paula had been with Jephson since the program's start. She was divorced, Jephson never married, and Alison was sure that Mrs. R would be only too happy to scratch whatever itches the great man might have.

The door to Jephson's inner office remained closed as Mrs. R talked on.

After almost two years of working for the man, Alison knew almost nothing about him personally. He was aloof, distant, a behaviorist with a mechanistic model of therapy that combined drugs with behavior modification.

At least, that was the operative assumption. Since his therapy sessions with the NGIs were conducted privately, no one else really knew what took place.

But a scenario was taking shape in her mind.

Many psychiatrists were reluctant to perform court-ordered evaluations, for good reason. The pay was almost nothing and the time demands great. The work itself was depressing and thankless, with grim prison visits and human beings at their worst. Trials and hearings were likely to bring attacks from attorneys, seeking to belittle professional competence and even verging into the personal.

But Jephson performed dozens of such evaluations per year, usually on cases that received no publicity. These almost never went to trial. They were settled at hearings among overworked, disinterested, state-appointed attorneys and judges.

Jephson's backup evaluations were usually performed by Vikram Ghose, a timid man from India who was on a continuously provisional status, without a license to practice independently in the United States, but whom Jephson had hired at Clevinger.

Suppose that, once in a while, the tumblers lined up to present low-profile cases, offenders with histories that suggested mental illness. These men screened by Jephson in private prehearing sessions. He then selecting, not the genuinely mentally ill, but sociopaths who might be keenly intelligent, especially in their own interest. Shading evaluations and obliquely coaching to present them as schizophrenic or bipolar.

Then guiding them through therapy, with information couched, coded, conveyed largely by emphasis, and absorbed by that instant, razor-keen intuition. The rules would be made immediately clear: act out once and you were in jeopardy; twice, and you went back to Atascadero or Vacaville, places that made Clevinger look like a Ramada Inn, to remain for years and maybe life. But stay in control, do twenty-plus months of soft time, and walk out free and clear. Therapy confidential. Negative feedback easily doctored and no central agency to correlate it. Especially if the men moved to other areas of the country, perhaps even changing identities.

"Sorry, dear," Mrs. R said, hanging up. "They know how to complicate things."

"Dr. Jephson asked to see me."

"Yes?" Mrs. R drew the syllable out into a question. Vermillion lips compressed, she picked up the phone again. She said, "Dr. Chapley's here," then looked up and nodded.

Jephson's private office possessed the flavor of a Cambridge don's, with its supplied grandeur overcoming the cheap, textured drywall and aluminum windows. The desk was his own, a massive structure of antique oak with blotting pad, inkstand, and a silver tray of stationery. A small TV/VCR unit for educational videos sat on a rollered stand in a corner. Several diplomas and awards hung on the wall behind him, flanked by thick volumes on neurology, psycho-analytic theory, and behavior modification, sit-ting shoulder to shoulder on shelves like haughty authorities.

"Alison," he said. "Please sit down."

He swiveled to the side and leaned back in the chair, slender hands clasping each other with a relaxation that seemed imposed.

"From time to time something comes along that makes me realize my shortcomings. Such as the poor follow-up on those NGIs that you brought to my attention. My focus has always been on results. I've let other aspects suffer, bureaucratic details and such. Our system is imperfect, our resources limited. One does the best one can."

He paused.

"It's a very impressive best, Dr. Jephson," she said. "No one would argue with that."

"I'm afraid I'm not much good at delegating responsibility, either."

This time she waited. Jephson's fingers steepled.

"I've been thinking for some time that JCOG would benefit from an administrative director," he said. "Someone to take over the day-to-day business, the hands-on operation."

Her eyebrows arched with comprehension. So: become a team player—and acquire the position of administrative director of JCOG. Stay another year or two, blind to what was going on, then carry the weight of that credential to wherever she wanted to go next.

From threat to bribe.

She said, "I think that's a wonderful idea. It would free you up for more important things."

He waved a hand modestly. "Just putting other talent to good use."

"Did you have anyone in particular in mind?"

Jephson swiveled back to her and smiled, a gift he bestowed rarely. "I shouldn't think I'd need to look too far from home."

"When would you be implementing this?"

"Oh, it will take a few months. We need a formal job description, funding, all that."

Or else it was a stall. Nothing definite

promised—but a way to keep her quiet until he could come up with something damaging to her.

She said, "I wouldn't call that poor follow-up a detail, Dr. Jephson. Those are dangerous men. No one knows where they are."

His smile remained, but his pale eyes went glacial. "I *am* looking into it, Alison."

She bit off the words, *So am I*, and stood.

"Keep me posted," she said.

Mrs. R was busy over a stack of papers. She waved beringed fingers as Alison walked by.

Alison paused at the outer door. "Paula, is John Garlick's release still on schedule?"

Mrs. R looked up, surprised. "As far as I know. Why?"

"I just wondered if any hitches had developed."

"You'd have to ask Dr. Jephson." Mrs. R's gaze returned to the papers.

Alison's gaze turned hard, anger flaring at being caught in this smug charade.

"Suppose Garlick stops reporting for meds?"

"The outpatient clinic would notify us," Mrs. R said.

"But that's that, right? Nobody else would know. Nobody'd go looking for him."

"Social workers would try to contact him."

"Meaning what? A phone call or two? What if he just disappeared?"

Mrs. R placed both hands flat on the desk and leaned forward.

"You wouldn't go looking for those men either, Alison. It's not like on the wards. You can't just scream for help."

Back on Three-Psych, Alison imagined a subtle shift among the staff she passed: gazes of curiosity or wariness. The patients looked different, too: sly and secretive instead of confused. She realized she was assessing them all in terms of: *Who might be in on this?*

The answer kept coming back: *Anyone*.

A few minutes before five P.M., Alison let the heavy door of Three-Psych swing closed behind her and walked out into the damp twilight air. The afternoon had included a Dual Diagnosis Group meeting, for patients with both mental illness and drug problems from fortified wine to inhaling propane.

Garlick, a one-time heavy drinker and meth user, had put in a mandatory appearance. Today, there was no baiting of other patients. He had been quiet, polite, his gaze rarely meeting hers, as if he had known he was under her scrutiny.

Soon to be released.

She opened the Mercedes' door and was swinging herself in when her mind registered what the car's interior light showed:

A small white box, lying on the driver's seat.

Her breath stopped. But a second later, she exhaled and managed a smile.

A return gift from Monks.

She left the door open for the light, and opened the box with her thumbnails. Under a layer of tissue paper lay a five-by-seven photograph. The setting was a forest clearing, with a thick growth of redwoods at its edges. The corner of a shed was visible, with a rusty corrugated iron roof.

In the foreground was the face of a man. He was looking over his left shoulder, his gaze fixed on the camera, his mouth slightly open. The sense was that he had been taken by surprise and was just realizing that the photographer was there. His eyes were shadowed beneath the bill of a baseball cap, but an ugly, unmistakable sense of menace emanated from them.

Recognition came to her with sick shock. He was Caymas Schulte, one of the phony NGIs, released a few months after she had started working at Clevinger; the only one she had personally known.

Her fingers felt rough edges on the photo's back. She turned it over.

Another picture was glued on that looked like it had been cut out of a book: a small pretty bird, with a red head and yellow and black markings. A cartoon-style balloon was drawn in ink, issuing from its mouth. It contained musical notes, as if the bird were singing.

Heart hammering, she swiveled to look around, as if the message-bearer might still be standing there. As if it might be the phantom lover from her childhood, whom she knew had touched her once, but she had no memory of.

Her twelfth summer, at the family's country house. An older cousin, Gerald, a gentle boy who teased her in a way she was beginning to understand.

Another boy who lived nearby: Earl Lipscomb, quiet, polite, but with something frightening in his eyes. She would see him in the distance when she was alone: feel him around her edges.

One early fall day, the two young men gone hunting together. Gerald shot, mistaken by Earl Lipscomb for a deer. The death ruled accidental.

A crowded cemetery on a muggy afternoon. The coffin about to be lowered. Men opening the lid to tuck in a bit of shroud.

Inside the blackness, a glimpse of white: Gerald's face.

Her gaze rising from there, of itself, to meet the eyes of Earl Lipscomb, far at the fringes of the crowd.

In that instant, the truth seared into her mind: that her cousin had taken her place.

Herself, dropping like stone in a dead faint.

Later she learned that she had been unconscious for several minutes. She remembered only the distant sense of a vast barren landscape, with herself on it. Far away at the horizon stood a sort of beacon, endlessly searching. She remembered it sweeping closer, the electrifying instant before contact, and then nothing more.

But whatever had happened during those lost

moments made the next months of her life unreal, a shadowy existence that she had reentered like an amnesia victim. And she knew that whatever had touched her had been looking for her ever since. It had colored everything: career, men, life.

She leaned forward to start the car. Her gaze caught the pale oval of her own face reflected in the rear-view mirror. Her hazel eyes, which a man had once told her caught sunlight and reflected it back in bursts, looked feverishly bright.

From another car, another pair of eyes watched the Mercedes back out and drive away. A hand moved to the ignition key, but then stopped.

It was so delicate a matter, one that no texts addressed: the purification of a vessel, laying to rest the one who was there and bringing forth the one who waited.

But clearly, they were already coming together.

6

On his way home, Monks stopped to buy groceries and liquor at a small store run by an extended Portuguese family, a quiet place with scarred wooden floors and counters and a fine pall of dust hanging in the air. It was a biweekly ritual, more expensive than the bigger supermarkets, but they kept a fine butcher counter and a wealth of other delicacies: toothsome sausages, pungent cheeses, and jars of tart pickled vegetables.

Moreover, there was the feeling that they had come to depend on his trade, ordered in Finlandia vodka especially for him, and that the family would dwindle in some obscure but significant way beyond money if he failed them. The elderly beret-wearing padrone, or his sturdy black-dressed wife, would thank Monks with a heavy accent, dark eyes seeming to measure his vice as he lifted the vodka bottles into his arms.

From there the journey was on two-lane roads, traffic thinning and pavement narrowing as he drove farther west toward the north Marin coast. The drizzle had thickened to rain. He paused at his mailbox, tugging free the usual accumulation of journals and junk. The house was seventy yards farther up a graveled drive, isolated from the road and neighbors by a thick second growth of redwood, live oak, and twisted snakelike madrones, their slick bark glistening in the wet.

Inside, he went straight to the cat food cupboard. A whirl of tumbling fur erupted across the kitchen, the skirmishing of children inside too long on a rainy day: the little calico his daughter had named Felicity, and Cesare Borgia, a scarred old black-coated felon who had been feral until Monks gradually won his trust. Omar, a blue Persian the size of a beagle, watched from the couch like an emperor for whose entertainment the battle was being staged. By all indications he had lain there since Monks's departure, without moving or noticing that his human was gone.

The fight ended with Felicity crowhopping across the floor, tail held stiffly down, while Cesare sat on the contested ground licking a paw. Monks noted that everyone had ended up closer to the food bowls. It was sheer extortion; a neighbor had fed them hours earlier. His ex-wife had been able to hold out against them, but he had long since stopped even pretending. He considered the selection and chose the Kultured Kat Kidney Entree, feeling it was appropriate to tomorrow's ASCLEP business, and divided two cans into three clean bowls, an arbitrary assignment since everyone stole from everyone else's.

Then he made his first drink. Finlandia vodka steamed as it spilled over ice, with a twist of just enough lemon to bring out the flavor. The taste was somewhere between a sweet kiss and a bite. He took drink and bottle to the shower, and later poured a second while he toweled dry. He dressed in a worn flannel shirt and jeans and refilled his glass.

The rain was drifting through the trees in sheets now. He started a fire in the wood stove. Then he flipped through the San Francisco phone directory until he found the number for Tierney's Pub on Taylor Street.

A voice heavy with brogue answered.

Monks said, "Dennis O'Dwyer, if he's in."

The background noise brought him a vivid picture of the long, copper-covered bar lined with men drinking pints of Guinness, reading newspapers, playing darts, arguing politics, conspiring for the IRA. Whatever they did for a living, it was their real business to know what was going on. Dennis's specialty was the insurance end of medicine. He had been a claims adjuster with ASCLEP for more than thirty years.

"It's Carroll Monks," he said when Dennis's whiskey voice came on.

"How are you, me boy?" It came out sounding like *buy*. At Tierney's, Dennis became more Irish with the hours. He was white-haired, thick-bodied, with a purplish nose, cheeks mottled with broken veins, and a vast lexicon of memory for people and events.

"I need to chat a minute," Monks said. "Is this a good time?"

"None better."

"Do you remember a big case, maybe twelve years ago? The Vandenard heir, they called him Robby, shot a man."

"Indeed I do."

"I'm interested in the psychiatrist who evaluated Robby. His name's Jephson."

"A Brit, isn't he?"

"Yes."

Dennis coughed expressively.

"He got Robby ruled mentally incompetent," Monks said. "There's reason to think the proceedings weren't straight. Did you hear anything like that?"

"It was no secret that Robby got preferential treatment. Like anything else with that kind of money, Carroll. A whiff of trouble, and there's experts flying in from all over the world, with price tags on them."

"Like Bernard Capaldi?"

"Like Bernard. He's retired now. Not in good health, I hear."

"Was there any suggestion that Jephson was bought too?"

"I'm trying to remember the context I heard his name in. There was a lot of buzz in the insurance game about that incident."

"There's a gold mine in your head, Den."

"More like a peat bog these days. Defense liability exposure, that was it. Fear of a wrongful death suit. But it never materialized."

"The Vandenards bought off the victim's widow."

"Say what you like, it's a good way to turn a witness friendly. I can't recall anything specific about Jephson. I'll nose around first thing tomorrow."

"Den, she, the widow, told us Robby was suspected of murdering his sister."

"There was speculation. People who knew the family. It was kept very quiet, of course. He was only a child."

"What about the rest of the family?"

"A grim story, lad. Robert Senior, Robby's father, had a stroke not long after. His wife died in the mid-eighties. It was given out as heart failure, but the rumor was an overdose of drugs and alcohol. She'd been in treatment centers. Heart-*break*, more likely.

"And that was the end of them, the main-line Vandenards. They were the darlings of the city when those children were young. There's a branch, cousins I believe, who've inherited the interests."

Monks was silent.

"This Jephson," Dennis said. "Is he in trouble with ASCLEP?"

"No."

"Shame. You'll be at the meeting tomorrow?"

"Yes."

"I'll let you know if I find anything."

Monks rang off, then got out his address book and called Alison Chapley, his fingers seeming to remember her number as he punched the buttons. Her machine answered.

He said, "I have news. Give me a call."

He refilled his glass, noting that the bottle was approaching a quarter empty: filtering through the microscopic labyrinths of liver and kidneys, alcohol molecules separated out and carried by the bloodstream to the hypothalamus to produce a temporary euphoria, followed by mass cell destruction high and low, a fast-forwarded kaleidoscope of frames to the body's dissolution. He considered the necessity of a kidney transplant, picturing donor organs like shy mollusks in the sea caves of the peritoneum, hiding from predatory human eyes and the rubber-gloved hands that probed to scoop them out, and wondered again if the malaria was coming on. He refilled his glass and went to check his supply of Plaquenil, a marginal remedy almost as bad as the disease.

When he came back, he paused at a photograph on the living room shelf: himself, his ex-wife Gail, their daughter Stephanie and son Glenn. Gail had remarried, to a professor of environmental studies at UC Davis. Stephanie was the good child, in her last year of pre-med there, staunch member of the swimming team. Glenn had last been heard from in Seattle, where he seemed to be making a career of skateboarding, panhandling, and drugs: a world of predators, with Glenn on his way to becoming one of them, or perhaps a victim.

They had been twelve and nine when the photo was taken: just about the same age spread as Robby Vandenard and his sister Katherine.

They were the darlings of the city when those children were young.

Sixteen years as husband and father, nine of them as chief of Emergency Services at the major trauma center of Bayview Hospital in Marin. The change seemed to have happened fast, but in fact it had been building for years: pressures that had grown subtly, pushing him into a series of decisions that were not major in themselves, but led him along until, like an electron forced from its orbit, he had made a quantum leap.

An incompetent internist whose negligence had allowed a man to die of a heart attack. A deep-pockets malpractice suit that named the Bayview ER and Monks as codefendants, although their performance had been exemplary.

The hospital administration's agreement to settle—a settlement which would have tarnished
Monks's name, linking him with the negligence—which he refused to accept. A growing
reputation as "not a team player," to which he
responded militantly against the good-old-boy
system of uncredentialed procedures. A growing
alienation from staff, colleagues, even felt by his
wife and children in the community.

Then one night a tense radio contact with a
team of paramedics in the field, attending an
elderly seizure victim. The senior of the medics
assuming it was a coronary, and preparing to give
a shot of adenosine—which Monks expressly
ordered *against*, fearing it would eliminate the
heart block that might be keeping the patient
alive. Argument. The sudden loss of radio contact for eight minutes from the medics' end.

Then the panicked report that the patient had
died.

The medics claiming that Monks had ordered
the shot.

And some time within the next twenty-four
hours, the radio tape—the only hard evidence of
what had actually happened—disappearing.

Monks stepped out on the deck and drank from
the bottle, a long pull that burned his mouth and
insides. With the rain slashing his face, he stood at
that too-familiar point of wanting never to stop, to
keep riding on the back of that fire-breathing
mount of alcohol that he had realized long ago he

would never entirely break, but could only fight a lifelong battle to keep in check.

The phone rang. Most nights, he would have let it go.

"Tell me your news," Alison said.

Monks told her.

She said, "There was nothing in Robby's file to suggest he'd murdered his sister. I'd have spotted that, trust me."

He stepped close to the wood stove so that it warmed the backs of his thighs.

"I see two possibilities," he said. "Jephson genuinely didn't know about that. Or he knew perfectly well that Robby was a dangerous son of a bitch, and he faked the diagnosis. Maybe that's how the whole thing got started. It worked so well with Robby, he kept going."

"I'm glad you found something. I kind of stuck my neck out today."

"How so?"

"Jephson offered me a bribe, or wanted me to think so. Administrative director of JCOG. I more or less threw it back in his face."

Monks massaged his temples with his fingertips.

"I'd advise a little more caution, Alison. This might make Jephson look foolish, but there's no evidence of anything criminal."

"Somebody knows something. They left a message in my car."

Monks said, "A *message*?"

"A photograph of one of those missing NGIs: Caymas Schulte." She described the incident with adolescent breathlessness.

"Was the car locked?"

"I guess I forgot."

"Very sloppy, Alison."

"I looked up the bird in a book," she said. "It's a Western Tanager. Caymas comes from a sort of Ma Barker clan up in the Mendocino woods. The mother's an old hippie, Haven Schulte. Three fathers for five kids. She gave them all nature names: Aspen, Mica, Dolphin. There's a boy about seventeen named Tanager."

Monks said, "Whoa. Slow down."

"It's an invitation," she said. "I'm supposed to go talk to Tanager."

"To Mendocino? Up in the backwoods? For Christ's sake. It's an invitation into an ambush."

"If somebody wanted to hurt me, why would they warn me? They could just take me out."

"Not quite as conveniently. Caymas is the one who raped and strangled the little boy?"

"Yes."

"Caught a searcher in a snare, hung him upside down, and almost beat him to death with a baseball bat? That guy?"

"Look, he scared the shit out of me, I admit it," she said. "Very quiet on the surface. Underneath—something else."

"He could be up there waiting for you, Alison. This could all be set up by Jephson."

"And it could be someone else at Clevinger who knows what's going on, but is scared to come forward. Knows Tanager can tell me something that would blow this open."

Monks drained his glass and walked to the refrigerator for more ice, tucking the phone between shoulder and ear.

"You'd be very foolish to go alone."

He could almost see her smile.

"I was hoping you'd say that."

Inside Monks's bedroom closet was a safe, bolted to the floor, where he kept his guns and a few valuables. He took out a 7-millimeter Beretta automatic and then, after a hesitation, an envelope of photographs. He set them on the dining room table along with weapon cleaning supplies: rods, swabs, oil. He had not fired the pistol in years, and never at a live target. Carrying it concealed was strictly illegal, but the law could be reasoned with.

He poured one more drink, put the bottle away, and cleaned the Beretta. When he was done, he washed his hands and opened the envelope of photos.

Alison had told him of their existence shortly after they had started seeing each other.

"I met this guy at a party. Before you," she added quickly. "A photographer. He begged me to pose. I thought, why not? He's a professional, right?"

"What kind of photos?" Monks said, already guessing.

"They started off straight, just sexy. Then went on from there."

"Went on how far?"

She shrugged. "We did a bunch of coke. I got worked up. There must have been a hidden camera."

Monks exhaled. "I'm sure it happens all the time."

"He sent me one. I can buy the rest. Would you come with me? I don't think he'd pull anything. I'd just feel—exposed all over again."

The photographer's name was Gary Benniger. He lived on a houseboat in Sausalito. He was in his early thirties, handsome, with perfect teeth, curled hair that appeared to have been tinted blond, and a shirt open halfway down his tanned chest. He was unctuously polite, maintaining the charade that these were photos Alison had commissioned. Monks watched silently while she exchanged two thousand dollars cash for the packet.

Monks said, "How do we know there are no copies?"

Benniger smiled, the smile of a man who had decided he no longer needed to pretend. "You her uncle?"

Monks took a photograph of his own from his coat pocket and tossed it on the floor at Benniger's feet. It was a black-and-white that had been taken by a navy journalist during the fighting around Quangtri. It showed Monks, years younger but clearly recognizable, on a hospital ship in the South China Sea, wearing bloody scrubs, staring haggardly at the next helicopter load of torn men on stretchers being rushed into surgery.

"Careful out there," Monks said. "Things can get rough."

On the way to the car, Alison said, "Still want to hang around with a bitch this dumb?"

"Somebody's going to have to keep you out of trouble."

She handed the packet of photos to him. They were color, glossy, professional quality. The first several showed her posed in, then removing, filmy bra and thong panties, leaving on white thigh-high stockings and a gold necklace. The next in the series was obviously taken from farther away and was less artfully staged. She was kneeling, caressing the erection of the man she faced. There were a dozen more, apparently taken at timed intervals of a minute or two.

"Look them over," she said, "and tell me where you want to start."

Monks went to the refrigerator and took out the evening's centerpiece, a thick filet mignon. The cats closed in like sharks, using his absence that day as leverage for tyranny. He distributed succulent bits of raw steak until the swirl of fur around his ankles turned to the more pressing business of paw-washing and naps, then put what was left on the hibachi.

He ate standing up in front of the wood stove: the filet charred just right, al dente linguine tossed with garlic and Parmesan, half an avocado soaked in vinegary blue-cheese dressing. The meal brought on fatigue from tension and lack of sleep. He imagined he could feel his blood pouring to his stomach to aid digestion, leaving his body like a deflated balloon. By the time he finished washing the dishes, he was in a half-dream. He walked down the hall to his bedroom. He put the photos back in the safe, but left the Beretta on his dresser, and fell into bed.

That time of the photographs incident had been a bad one in most other ways. His career was damaged, his marriage over. He was drinking far too much and not caring about what was left, with a harsh destructive anger turned inward.

One night several weeks later, Alison had whispered: "I want you to choke me a little. Not too hard. Not enough to bruise."

He knew that professionally, she specialized in violence. She was working on the psychiatric ward at Letterman, San Francisco's major VA hospital, and sometimes went into San Quentin to teach anger management groups. But this was the first time he had seen it spill over into personal life.

It made Monks uneasy and he resisted at first,

but then he pleased her. What he had not imagined was the intensity it would bring to him, too. As the nights passed, the limits stretched, and Monks began to realize that he was caught in an obsession.

There were no promises of fidelity between them. As more weeks passed, another phase began, whether deliberate or careless on her part, he could not tell: hints of other affairs, half-overheard phone calls, unexplained absences. Every week or two, he would come out to the Bronco to find a gift on the seat, leaving him to guess whether it was tease, or apology, or reward.

One late afternoon he finished a shift at Mercy Hospital and came out to find a black silk scarf embroidered with gold. He stopped by her house on his way home. She was not there. Monks started drinking. Over the next hours he reached a strange disconnected clarity, his reflexes as sharp as a surgeon's, or so it seemed.

When her headlights lit the window, he waited inside the front door, and when she came in, he pinned her against it and slipped the scarf around her throat. She shuddered, sinking beneath his weight to the floor.

And Lord, something thickened around them like a black whirlpool, turning into an entity that had a life of its own, terrifying and ravenous. Its force filled him like talons operating a puppet, like electricity surging through a man helpless to let go of a live wire. His hands tightened, while her own sounds and clutching fingers seemed not to fight but to urge him on.

She was almost quiet when he tore himself free and stumbled away like a felon into the night.

From there Monks had started to turn back the way he had come, to relative respectability, sobriety, a stable life. A new force had arisen to drive him, more powerful than any yet: fear.

But not of what had happened, or even of what he now knew he was capable of. He was afraid because that had been the most intimate moment of his life.

The cats were prowling now in the dark, shadows moving continually at the edges of his vision, as if there were dozens instead of just three. Soon they would join him, miffed that he had been gone, but too glad he was back to miss the chance. Tonight, with luck and the blessed combination of exhaustion and alcohol, he would not wake and toss.

Monks, a name traceable back to the ninth century in Ireland's northwest, from the Gaelic *manachan*: a monk, a solitary, one who lived alone.

7

A few minutes before 10 A.M. the next day, Monks walked down Montgomery Street in the San Francisco financial district, a sunless corridor with austere old edifices that stood like a row of cathedrals to wealth. He turned into a granite-faced structure with a brass plaque that read THE CHILDERS BUILDING.

The lobby was high-ceilinged, discreetly elegant, hung with tapestries and portraits of substantial men. A security guard greeted Monks with measured deference, suggesting that while he might be presentable, he was no one of consequence. Monks stepped off the elevator at the seventh floor, then walked along a burgundy-carpeted, walnut-wainscotted hallway, past heavy doors embossed with gold-leaf business escutcheons, to the offices of ASCLEP. He was greeted by a secretary whose acquaintance he had never made further than the name Kristin. She was young, pretty, fashion conscious, and her smile always seemed to pity him for any number of things, beginning with his age.

Dennis O'Dwyer was standing just inside the door of the conference room, as if he had been waiting.

"I dug up a tasty little bit on your man Jephson," he said quietly. "Stick around after."

Monks nodded and took his seat at the long oval table, beside Dennis, Stover Larrabee, and ASCLEP'S attorney, Clarisse Kressler.

At the other end of the table, a kidney specialist named Jerome DeMers and his attorney faced them like an opposing tag team.

ASCLEP, named for the god of healing, was a doctor-owned malpractice insurance company. In the 1970s, the deep-pockets game had started running wild: attorneys cast lawsuits like fishing nets and juries awarded fantastic settlements in personal injury cases, irrespective of anything resembling common sense. Malpractice insurance rates climbed sharply even for physicians with pristine records and were on their way to becoming astronomical. Most companies simply passed the increased cost on, but for ASCLEP, this would be passing it on to themselves.

Thus, what was known as the ASCLEP Performance Evaluation Board came into being: a group of medical professionals, attorneys, and insurance executives who forestalled as much trouble as they could before it ran them into the ground. When an insuree was sued for malpractice, the board reviewed the case and made a recommendation as to whether ASCLEP should go to court or settle. Unlike most companies, ASCLEP would fight if they were convinced their physician was in the right, even at greatly increased expense.

Less frequently came situations where there was reason to believe an insuree was a risk. If this was confirmed, his insurance was dropped. This was much disliked by defense attorneys and was frequently challenged, along with the board's murky status in general. It was not the sort of peer review conducted by state and county medical societies. It did not officially determine whether malpractice had occurred, did not exonerate or censure. It was not a legal organization and made no recommendations to any enforcing body. Its proceedings were absolutely private, except in the rare instances when a defending physician's anger overcame his common sense.

Today, Monks thought, might just be one of those days.

Dr. DeMers was a big man, handsome, dressed in a well-tailored navy blazer and pleated charcoal slacks, with a red-striped silk tie just loose at the neck. His black hair glistened with mousse. DeMers, Larrabee had discovered, liked the good life, including gambling cruises on Lake Tahoe.

Clarisse moved to the room's central area, which served as a sort of demilitarized zone. She was a sultry dark blond in her late thirties, a trifle broad-beamed, but attractive. She was known as Clarisse the Piece, a name, or title, Monks had once heard her referred to, in her presence, at a company-sponsored dinner. He had frozen in the expectation of fury, but she had not seemed to mind at all—on the contrary.

Clarisse repeated the alarum that began each meeting like the company's private Miranda Rights reading.

"Gentlemen, let me impress upon you the need for confidentiality. It's very much in everyone's interest. Any breach might make proceedings vulnerable to outside scrutiny and cause litigation against both parties.

"It's ASCLEP's concern that Dr. DeMers has acted in violation of ethics, good judgment, and law. Specifically, we have reason to believe that he falsified data for Mrs. William Edgery in order to move her onto a priority list for a kidney transplant."

DeMers's attorney, one Corbin Rydell, leaned forward with his forearms on the table. A briefcase rested beside him like a nuclear weapon. Over the years, Monks had become something of a connoisseur of defense approaches, ranging from a cozy,

We're-all-in-this-together routine, to the blazing outrage of You're-going-to-regret-the-day-you-were-ever-born. This one he quickly identified as the always fashionable, restrained but menacing, Gentlemen-you-are-wasting-my-valuable-time riff. It was unfortunately undercut by plump cheeks and an upturned nose, giving Rydell a somewhat porcine look.

Rydell said, "I'll start by pointing out that this board has no legal jurisdiction."

"We'll all aware of that, Mr. Rydell," Clarisse said. "This is an informal proceeding. To which your client agreed."

"And that a specialist being evaluated by an emergency physician is preposterous."

"Dr. Monks acts as chair, not as judge. Although I'll point out that he's nationally board-certified in internal medicine as well as emergency medicine."

Monks held his hand up for silence.

"We have statements from several specialists, Mr. Rydell. The chief surgeon who performed the transplant on Mrs. Edgery, for openers." He took a sheaf of papers from his daypack, and several more silent presences entered the fray: more potential salvoes in the battle to sink this little ship.

"What you've provided me so far is pure speculation." Rydell paused, the stare sweeping them one at a time. "No lawsuit has been filed. There's no statement from Mrs. Edgery herself, no hard evidence and no witnesses. Only what amounts to unsubstantiated rumor."

DeMers listened with a faint, stony smile.

"He didn't just falsify data," Monks said. "He deliberately sclerosed the veins around at least one of Mrs. Edgery's dialysis shunts, and probably others before it."

Rydell leaned sharply forward, as if about to lunge out of his seat.

"That's a hell of a serious charge, Dr. Monks, and like the rest of it, completely unsubstantiated."

This had started several months earlier, with ASCLEP being contacted by a sharp-eyed surgeon named Becker, chief of a team of transplant specialists. Mrs. Edgery was fifty-five, the wife of an oil executive, living in the quietly posh town of Atherton. She had been stably undergoing dialysis for over two years under DeMers's care, when her shunt—an artificial passage between artery and vein, allowing the introduction of blood-filtering needles—suddenly clotted. A new shunt was created, and four months later, it clotted as well.

This allowed the patient to be categorized as having difficult vascular access, and therefore eligible for the next available organ that matched her tissue and blood types. The problem was that there were hundreds of other hopeful recipients who might already have been waiting years and might be forced to wait years longer, wearing beepers twenty-four hours a day, ready to rush at a minute's notice to a hospital or even airport. Mrs. Edgery had leapfrogged to the top of the list.

Dr. Becker had become uneasy for no reason he could pin down. Then, examining her after the transplant operation, he noticed an atypical hardening of the vascular tissue around the shunt. He went back over the records and came away further dissatisfied. There was nothing concrete—DeMers had covered his tracks by showing rising blood urea nitrogen and creatinine levels on his charts—but the sudden jumps had no clear cause and did not jibe with the patient's previous history.

The surmise was that DeMers had intimated to Mrs. Edgery that her transplant could be expedited, and in return for a payoff, had injected the veins surrounding the shunt with a sclerosing solution of the type used in healing hemorrhoids, causing them to close off. And that DeMers had done the same thing with previous patients, perhaps several, in order to support a lifestyle best described as glossy.

But Rydell was right. There was no way to prove this scenario. The surgeons' suspicions were only that, and the irregularities were not conclusive. DeMers, Monks admitted, was slick.

Rydell sat back. "I assume it's clear that the withdrawal of insurance would be extremely damaging to my client, both materially and in terms of reputation. We'd have to strongly consider the possibility of suing ASCLEP."

Larrabee had been chain-drinking coffee from a Styrofoam cup, looking as if his mind was on something else. He crumpled the cup with an abrupt popping sound that startled everyone.

He said, "On April 11, 1996, William Edgery made a fifty thousand dollar cash withdrawal from the Union Street Wells Fargo branch in San Francisco. Just three weeks before Mrs. Edgery's first shunt malfunction."

Monks watched DeMers. His face stayed firm but his skin was turning a curious gray, almost blue.

"On July 17, Mr. Edgery made a second fifty thousand dollar withdrawal, this time from a branch in Sacramento. Her second shunt malfunction came two weeks after that."

"Objection—"

"This is not a courtroom, Counselor," Larrabee said. "Your objections don't mean dick."

"There's no evidence of any connection."

"The Edgerys refused to be interviewed by me. But they'd talk to the IRS. There'll be a paper trail. There always is."

Rydell gave the hard stare a brief try, but it faltered.

"What's next, Doc?" Larrabee said to DeMers. "Kidney guys who aren't too fussy are in big demand down in Mexico. China, too. I hear they're parting out prisoners over there."

DeMers stood with a sudden violent movement, shoving his chair back.

"My job is to have my patients up walking around. Not wired to a dialysis machine." He glowered for seconds longer, a large and angry man in a small room, then wheeled and stalked out, slamming the door.

Monks said, "A hundred grand. Not a bad little tip for a few hours' work."

"I don't know how you got that information, Larrabee," Rydell said venomously, "but it wasn't legal. It remains irrelevant in my mind."

Monks stood, walked to Rydell, and leaned close. "How does it feel, to make a career of lying?"

He felt something touch his arm: Larrabee's hand. Rydell, tightlipped, stacked papers into his briefcase, his visible composure recovered.

An utter unconcern for the right and wrong of the situation, Monks thought: only anger because you've lost. He thought, we enjoy the highest standard of medical care in history. That standard depends on responsible attorneys protecting responsible physicians, and weeding out the scumbags like DeMers.

Then there's the ones like you. When did this figure become an American hero, this bureaucrat with a briefcase who makes a rich living by picking laws apart to confound justice? Who never takes a genuine risk, who contributes nothing of real worth, who has all the time and resources in the world to erect a legal structure that nurtures him and his cronies?

Monks thought, I make a hundred serious decisions every shift I pull in the Emergency Room, with a significant percentage of them walking the edge of life or death. One mistake, and hordes of sycophants like you are all over me. When *you* make a mistake, you just add it to your bill at five hundred dollars an hour. If I charge a patient half that, total, I've saved him acute misery and maybe his life.

It breaks my heart, he thought, that I can't prosecute that son of a bitch DeMers and you along with him. If it were up to me, his next procedure would be in San Quentin, and you'd be mopping the floor.

Monks said, "If your client walks into this room again, there'll be a legal secretary here from Richard Cook Associates, recording an official transcript. I'll deliver it to the county attorney's office myself. I'm sure I don't need to remind a man of your standing that tampering with medical records is a felony."

Rydell clamped his briefcase shut, stood, and without speaking, left the room.

"He's thinking, go ahead, knock yourself out," Larrabee said. "There's money in it for him every step of the way."

Dennis O'Dwyer sat back in his chair with the relief of a man who had just found out his tumor was benign. DeMers might never have gotten caught, but if he had, it would probably have cost ASCLEP several million dollars. As it was, no information would be passed on to competitors, but any other insurance company would know damned well that ASCLEP had not dropped him for nothing. The best hope was that he would not be able to get more insurance, or the rates would be so ruinous he would be driven out of practice. And if he did keep practicing medicine, other watchdog agencies would be tipped off by this; he would probably be too nervous to try a stunt like that again.

It was not enough, but it was better than nothing.

"I appreciate your sense of theatrics, Stover," Clarisse said reproachfully, "but you might have told me about the payoffs a little earlier. I spent two days getting ready to fist-fight Rydell."

"I didn't want to compromise you, Clarisse. The counselor was right, I got that information in a highly illegal fashion."

"Bullshit."

"No, really. A pal at Wells Fargo. It's going to cost the company a bottle of single malt Scotch."

"I meant about you protecting my virtue." There was a brief silence while the men did not look at each other. "Is that true, about China?"

"It's a persistent rumor."

Monks stood, catching Larrabee's eye. They walked with Dennis out to the hall.

Dennis said, "This Jephson. When he treated

Robby Vandenard for killing that fellow in '84, that wasn't the first time. The Vandenards brought him in to evaluate Robby clear back in '71, when his sister was killed. Sealed records, all that. Robby was sent to live with relatives in South Africa immediately after."

Larrabee said, "So Jephson was covering for Robby even when he was a kid."

Monks remembered the news photo of Robby Vandenard, the age in the eyes of the man who had taken two lives, and then his own, starting at the age of eleven.

Monks said, "I don't think he was ever a kid."

Monks cruised slowly up Lokoya Road, in the mountains between Napa and Sonoma, following the crude map Darla Lutey had drawn to the old Vandenard estate. It was at the road's end, well removed from neighbors. The black iron fence was thickly overgrown with brush, the gate locked with a chain. There was just enough space for him to slip through.

He walked up a worn asphalt lane, with unkempt tree limbs closing off the sky overhead and crowding the edges. He had gone a good quarter of a mile before the vista opened up again. Steep hills rose on both sides, cresting into a ridge of cliffs ahead. The lower slopes were lush with neglected vineyards. There was a scattering of buildings: a stone caretaker's cottage, and some sheds, all looking disused.

And a three-story Victorian mansion that would have been a picture of elegance except for peeling paint and boarded windows.

A pair of heavy plank doors had been cut into the base of the cliffs. Monks walked to them. They were locked with a rusted iron hasp that looked hand-forged. Behind them would be the wine cellar, where the Vandenards in years past had laid in their private supply, grown and bottled on the estate by the old Italian hands.

Where Katherine Vandenard, aged fourteen, had been alone one afternoon in the summer of 1971. Until someone came in after her with a grape-picker's knife.

Fog lay close to the ground, clinging to the neglected vines like crêpe. The sky was a streaked and moving tapestry of gray. The place was on the way to Mendocino, and Monks had decided to stop, in the vague hope of finding someone who might have more light to shed on whatever had happened between Robby Vandenard and Francis Jephson. Or perhaps, really, to pay respects to the girl whose death was the germinal event in all this.

He turned to go and stopped. A man was walking toward him from the caretaker's house. Now Monks could see smoke from the chimney, barely visible against the mist.

Monks said, "I realize I'm trespassing. I apologize."

"You want to show me some ID?" He was lean,

bearded, wearing the uniform of men of his type: jeans, work boots, and baseball cap pulled low. At a guess, he was about Monks's age, beard graying, face heavily weathered, hard-eyed, a man life had not been kind to. He spoke with a twang that brought to mind Larrabee's words about Merle Lutey: *That's got Okie written all over it.*

Monks handed over his driver's license. "Are you the owner?"

The caretaker examined the license.

"Nope," he said, handing it back. "Mind telling me what you're doing here?"

"I've got some business involving the Vandenard family. I thought there might be somebody around who knew them."

"Place is owned by an investment group down in the city. I'm just here till they get their price. Don't know who had it before that."

"Sorry to disturb you."

"No problem. Truth to tell, it gets kind of lonesome."

"I could see that," Monks said. "Well. I'll be going."

"What kind of doctor?"

Monks turned back, fearing that he might become trapped in a conversation about this hermit's ailments.

"Emergency," he said.

"Must take good nerves."

"They're not as good as they used to be."

The caretaker's chin lifted slightly, a gesture

that seemed to mean he was satisfied.

Back in the Bronco, Monks consulted a map of the area. The town of Calistoga was roughly twenty miles north. It seemed quite a coincidence that Francis Jephson had been hiking in this area, and bitten by a rattlesnake, a few weeks after Katherine Vandenard's death.

Unless he had really been *here*, on the Vandenards' estate, and the location of the snakebite incident had been falsified in order to hush up the reason: to evaluate Robby.

Monks drove back down into the Napa Valley and turned north on Highway 29 toward Mendocino.

8

Monks waited for Alison Chapley in the parking lot of the Mendocino Headlands Inn, an older place built on a bluff overlooking the Pacific. The horizon was still light, and the surf breaking on the great ochre rocks threw up rainbows of iridescent spray; but in the redwood forests that sloped up from the coast, night had come.

They had driven their own cars and checked into separate rooms. Neither had suggested otherwise.

The motel door opened. She hurried to the Bronco, wrapped in a dark raincoat and scarf, carrying a large woven hemp bag.

"North on Highway One," she said. "There's a turnoff in a couple of miles."

He drove through the streets of Fort Bragg, a town of several thousand with a harbor at the south end and a lumber mill taking up most of the north. The demographics were noticeably different than in the Bay Area: loggers, fishermen, pony-tailed ghosts of the sixties, driving vintage American pickup trucks.

She turned toward him in the seat, her back against the door.

"Thanks. This would have been tough, alone."

"It still doesn't feel easy."

"Easier."

The road that led to the Schulte homestead turned inland, a steep series of switchbacks sparsely lined with houses. It quickly became closed in with forest, dripping with mist.

"I didn't have time to change," she said. "Do you mind?"

He glanced over. She was unbuttoning the raincoat. He caught a glimpse of skin, with brief black bands at breasts and hips, and pulled his attention back to the winding road.

"No. I don't mind."

"It should be another few miles. Box 1382." She took something from her bag and leaned forward, then came up more slowly, fingers working their way along her calves, pulling on gray tights.

Monks said, "How do you want to handle this?"

She shifted in the seat, with the sound of snapping elastic.

"Tanager's seventeen. He's been held back in school. Maybe he's a little slow. Maybe because of everything that's happened with Caymas." She was taking something else from the bag, unfolding it. "I don't want him to think we're from the hospital, at least at first. I'm guessing he's just trying to hide and get through it all. If we come at him officially he might freeze up. I'll try to start him talking and see where it goes."

"If we're not us, then who are we?"

"We're spreading the word of the Lord." She smoothed a dress over her front, raising knees and then rump to pull it on. It was denim of a medium blue color, loose-fitting, calf-length.

"You think that's fair to the kid?"

With sudden sharpness, she said, "I don't think there's anything fair about any of this. Zip me up."

Monks did, fingers fumbling along the bumps of her spine. She retied the scarf with quick jerky motions. It was dark blue, bringing out the pallor of her face, and he realized she was not wearing makeup.

"I'm not much of an actor."

"You'll do fine," she said, more kindly. "You don't have to talk. Just look stern."

The fog was thickening, their headlights creating a tunnel, barely penetrating in some pockets. There were no signs of habitation now except for an occasional dirt road entrance marked by a mailbox.

He said, "Long way for a preacher to come calling."

"The Lord loveth not the spirit that is weak."

He smiled. Clearly, she had been doing her homework.

"I heard you were getting married," he said. "A couple years back."

She leaned her head against the window, lips twisting briefly.

"Matthew," she said. "A rising star in the investment world. He wanted me to quit my job. Move to a safe clean suburb of the mind, away from the slums where the poor people live. You?"

"Gail and I stay in touch." While he had never thought of it in those terms, his ex, had moved to that suburb, too.

"You told me once she'd decided you were bad luck, and she was afraid it would rub off."

He said, "Chances are she was right."

Abruptly, Monks braked hard. A small burly shape was ambling down the road's center toward them, making no effort to budge. As he skirted it, the headlights picked out a badger's white mask: beasts that would fight to the death before giving ground.

He said, "How hard have they tried to find Caymas?"

"He was scheduled to report to the outpatient clinic in Ukiah for decanoate injections twice a month. Stopped showing up more than a year ago. His family said he'd disappeared. He's a registered child molester, not allowed to leave the area. There's a bench warrant out for him."

"But nobody's looking?"

"They never do. Everybody's glad those men are someone else's problem." She took out a cigarette and held it. With the scarf and dress, it gave her the look of an actress in a Western movie, taking a break. Monks reached to push in the lighter, but she shook her head.

"I don't want it on my breath," she said. "He was attractive to kids—Caymas. Isn't that strange? The perfect older playmate. Always knew the right thing to say, to coax a child into playing a game. Keeping a secret. Most of the NGIs are scary. But I've only met a couple like him."

"If we did happen to run into him, you'd recognize him?"

"He's not somebody you forget."

Monks's right hand moved to his coat pocket, touching the Beretta. In a worst-case scenario, it just might provide the leverage to get them out of there.

He corrected himself. Worst case was that Caymas would have to dig a hole big enough for two bodies, not one, back in the dank redwood forests.

"Dennis O'Dwyer heard a rumor that when Robby Vandenard was a kid, they couldn't keep pets around," Monks said. "They'd end up dead."

"It all fits with what's been creeping up on me, about Robby. Men like him almost never commit suicide."

Monks drove a distance further before the implication hit him. When he turned, she was watching him patiently.

"Robby had a lot of nasty stuff on Jephson," she said. "I'm not saying Jephson had him killed, but I bet he didn't weep at the news."

Two miles later the headlights found the number, hand-painted in red on a battered mailbox shaped like a small Quonset hut. A dirt road led into the woods. They followed it two hundred yards before it curved to reveal a sprawling, wood-sided house with lit windows and smoking chimney.

Several vehicles were parked in no apparent order: pickup trucks, a dark customized van on its way to being trashed, a newish mini-station wagon, a fifties-era ton-and-a-half with wooden slat side racks and a flattened tire that made it list to one side. The shapes of other buildings, sheds and shacks and a looming hulk that might have been a barn, merged into the darkness beyond, with a few lights visible in the distance. The overwhelming sense was of a compound of hostiles.

The bark of a large dog boomed out, instantly picked up by others. Several low shapes appeared on the run, big black and yellow mutts with bared teeth and bristled spines, lunging through the light cast by the headlamps.

The front door of the house opened. There was no porch light: only a shadowed shape just visible, waiting inside. They got out, Alison fending off the growling dogs swarming her legs and thrusting noses in her crotch. She walked ahead of Monks to the porch, a hand purse clasped in front of her.

The woman waiting for them was in her fifties, buxom, well-preserved, wearing a multicolored peasant skirt. This would be the brood mare, Monks thought: Haven Schulte. One hand was on her hip, the other out of sight, as if gripping the barrel of a shotgun. Behind her came the sound of a television, voices and laugh track suggesting a sitcom. Another shape appeared behind her: a man, younger, watching them intently. He turned and spoke to someone unseen in the house. Monks felt a drop of sweat from his right armpit hit his flank. It was very cold.

"I *am* sorry to disturb you good people," Alison said. Her accent had gone unobtrusively Southern. "I'm Sister Helen and this is Brother Roy. We're from the First Denominational Pentecostal Church of Santa Rosa, and we've come to call on—" She opened a slip of paper and squinted at it in the dimness. "Tanager Shoo—Shool—"

Haven Schulte said wearily, "We've told you everything we have to tell you."

"Ma'am?"

"You're cops, right?"

"No'm," Alison said, puzzled. "We leave collection boxes in public places. People fill out forms asking to talk to us. To bring the Lord into their lives." She held the slip of paper up tentatively.

Haven Schulte's gaze remained on her several seconds longer, then moved to Monks. He was having no trouble looking somber.

Over her shoulder, Haven said, "Get your brother."

The man behind her walked outside, brushing past Monks with careful insolence. He was in his late twenties, with lank stringy hair and a presence thick enough for Monks to feel. The dogs fell in with him as he disappeared into shadow toward the compound's rear.

"We have some literature we'd like to leave with you," Alison said, opening her purse. She took out several pamphlets and offered them forward, but Haven folded her arms.

"You can wait here." She turned and went back in the direction of her interrupted TV show.

The night was peaceful and had a pleasant chill, with the soothing scent of pine smoke lacing the air. It brought Monks an abrupt memory of camping in the Sierras with Gail and the kids, all of them still young.

He kept his gaze centered on nothing, alert for movement at the edges, listening hard.

Minutes later, he picked out human footsteps among the patter of dog paws before the figures came into sight. The brother who had gone was back followed by a teenaged boy wearing huge baggy shorts and a knee-length T-shirt with a down vest over it, an outfit that made him look at the same time knobby and shapeless. His hair was cut floppy on top and close on the sides. His face was an unformed white oval that expressed bewilderment.

Tanager. Just about the same age, Monks realized, as his own son.

"I didn't fill out any paper," Tanager said. The brother, on his way back inside, stopped and waited just at the point where the dim light faded to shadow.

"It might have been someone else, thinking of you," Alison said quickly. "Somebody you might not even know cares about you. We're not asking you for anything. We just thought you might want to talk a minute." She turned to the older brother. "The rest of your family too, if they'd like. The Lord can light up a dark night like this."

He gave a throaty barking laugh and climbed the porch stairs, boot heels coming down with emphasis. The dogs followed him to the door, then milled uncertainly.

"Somebody who might think you're lonesome," Alison said to Tanager. She moved closer to him, her face earnest and concerned, a teenaged boy's wet dream, if marred somewhat by the presence of Monks and, perhaps, Jesus. "We all have things that hurt us, that we feel like we can't tell anybody."

Monks tried to look compassionate, which under other circumstances would have been easy. He held the doorway at the edge of his sight. There was no one visible now. Whoever the brother had spoken to had never appeared. Might still be in the house. Might have gone out a back door into the night.

More quietly, Alison said, "That person who cares about you? She put her name on this paper."

Tanager's gaze turned surprised. "Who?"

Alison shivered. "I'd love a chance to warm up, just for a minute. Do you have a room?"

Tanager lowered his head with shy pride. "I have my own cabin. With a stove."

Alison smiled.

They followed the boy past the rear of the house, where uncurtained windows gave a view of a large kitchen, empty of humans, with dishes stacked on the drainboard. The dirt path led on past a rail-fenced corral. Snufflings and a musty odor suggested horses or pigs. After that came an aging single-wide trailer, with paint shedding in patches from ridged aluminum siding. The windows gave off the blue-white light of another television. On a couch watching it sat two young men with a girl between them. She looked to be about fourteen years old and about seven months pregnant.

Ahead another fifty yards, standing alone, the

shape of a small cabin with a single lit window was coming visible. The path narrowed to a foot trail through the dense trees. Monks restrained his body's urge to pant.

"You live out here by yourself?" Alison said.

"Nobody else wants it. It's too far and there's no plumbing."

"You must be very brave. I'd be scared to death."

"I fixed it up," Tanager said with sudden eagerness. He opened the door. The spreading light revealed old rough-sawn board-and-batten siding that had been patched with newer wood. The door and window trim were freshly painted, a hopeful red. A shed roof extended out a few feet from one wall, protecting a stack of firewood and the carefully tarped shape of a motorcycle.

The inside was a single small room with a bunk, a few shelves of books, a small boom box, and a Nintendo game on the screen of a small TV. A large poster of Michael Jordan was tacked above an old school desk, stacked with high school texts and papers. It was a world, a sanctuary, and it cried out his need to escape.

One corner was lined with galvanized sheet metal, with a sheepherder's stove set on a brick hearth. The aged black iron radiated heat and the wood inside crackled comfortingly. Alison stepped toward it. Monks remained by the door, doing his best to stay invisible.

"That feels wonderful," she sighed. "I can't believe you fixed this place up yourself. How long did it take you?"

Tanager's gaze shifted awkwardly around the room, not quite meeting hers. His face was round, unformed, just beginning to sprout brindle whiskers.

"A couple months. My brothers helped with some stuff."

"I'll bet your girlfriends love it."

His face reddened with pleased embarrassment. "Not really."

"Come on. Have you asked anybody up here?"

"No," he said, the word half-swallowed.

"Well, they would."

Monks smiled gravely, senses bristling for the stealthy footstep, the shadow crossing the window.

"Lord, now I'm starving," she said. She took a Cadbury chocolate bar from her purse, broke it, and offered half to Tanager. He accepted with mumbled thanks.

"Are you nervous about asking girls out?"

He nodded, eyes downcast.

"Let me tell you something. Girls like boys who're shy. It means there's somebody important underneath. They want to get to know you, who you really are. Go for walks. Listen to music. Just talk. You'll find out."

Mouth full of chocolate, Tanager watched her hopefully, not seeming to find it bizarre that a pretty missionary was giving him advice on how to get laid.

"You said somebody put their name on that paper?"

She nodded. "Can you guess who?"

Her tone was subtly different: the teasing still there, but betraying tension. Tanager's face went wary.

"All right," she said. "Here."

She held out the slip of paper. He stepped to her hesitantly and took it. His lips moved to silently pronounce the name:

Alison.

He looked up swiftly, now alarmed.

"Don't be scared, Tanager," she said. She moved toward him a step. "Tell me who Alison is."

"I don't know."

"Is she a girl who likes you?"

He shook his head.

"Why does that name make you nervous? Did somebody give you a message? Something you're supposed to tell Alison?"

She took another slow step, as if she were trying to gentle a colt, hand outstretched.

"You can tell me. Because I'm Alison. I'm not from any church, Tanager. I'm a doctor. I worked with your brother Caymas."

He jerked away from her touch, eyes glistening. "You lied."

"I didn't want to scare you," she said quickly.

"I'll leave if you want, but I think you have something to tell me. Is it about Caymas? Do you know what happened to him?"

"He's at the hospital!"

"No, he's not. I work there. I'd know."

Tanager broke at that, bolting for the door, running into the night as if fleeing from the sheaf of light that spilled out.

Or from Alison's words, calling after him:

"Caymas hurt you too, *didn't* he?"

For half a minute she stood without moving. Monks waited with her, listening, staring into the dark.

Then she said softly, "Come back, Tanager." She stepped to the desk and scribbled something on a sheet of notebook paper.

Monks went first on the path this time. They were almost past the trailer, the figures still unmoving on the couch, when he heard Alison suck in her breath. He spun around. Something had appeared in a darkened window beside them, a pale oval, a face. Monks's fingers tugged with idiot clumsiness at the pistol.

Then stopped. The face was ancient, wrinkled, its mouth a toothless black gap which, he realized, was smiling. He glimpsed through the glass a tiny room, lit by a plastic statue of Christ opening His breast to expose a glowing crimson heart. There was a mattress on the floor, along with a tray containing a partial glass of milk and a bowl of what looked like baby food.

He did his best to smile back, and raised a hand in greeting. They moved along the silent path to the Bronco, where the dogs discovered them all over again, but no human presence came forward.

Out on the road, she pulled off the scarf, shook out her hair, then lit up a cigarette.

"I've been wanting one of these." She rolled down her window to exhale. A rush of air blew through the vehicle, touching the sweaty back of his neck. "That too cold?"

"It feels good." His gaze flicked restlessly to the mirror, watching for headlights. He recalled that locals sometimes knew these roads well enough to cruise without them.

"I've got a bottle of Finlandia in my room. Join me?" She was gazing straight ahead.

Monks said, "I could use a drink."

They did not speak again until they reached the motel.

Monks drank icy vodka, watching her undress. She took her time, making sure he saw. She looked unchanged, breasts heavy and rose-nippled, belly with a slight curve, full hips and strong thighs, a body that embraced with effortless power.

Finished, she sat back against the bedboard, knees drawn up, and reached for her own glass of wine.

"You just going to sit there?"

"For a minute," Monks said. "You would, too."

She laughed and stretched luxuriously, like a cat inviting play.

"I miss your cock."

He stood and came to sit in the curve of her body. Her arms went around him, fingers tugging at his shirt buttons. Monks leaned over and inhaled her scent from the soft place where her neck met her shoulder. He scraped her nipples lightly with his teeth, then harder, and moved on down, delicate flesh parting under his tongue with a faint acidic taste until she twisted, gasped, and lay still.

"I missed that, too," she said. "Come here."

Together they pulled off the rest of his clothes. She pushed him onto his back and crouched over him. Monks gazed back into her fierce eyes, amazed at the power this mysterious creature held over him.

She started to move, and thought left his mind.

9

Monks shifted carefully in the room's interior twilight. He lay on his back, his left arm around Alison. She had gone quiet, perhaps sleeping.

The worries of the day were rising in his mind again, quickly compounding themselves. But her hair was fragrant, her cheek warm against his skin, and his hand just fit in the curve of her waist. He waited, savoring again the last minutes: her astride him, hands on his chest, eyes closed, teeth biting her lower lip, hips moving slowly.

He rolled his head toward the sliding door onto the balcony, aware of a bit of sensory data out of place, like a subliminal but jarring sound. Light from the parking lot filtered in through the translucent curtain, outlining a squat shadow shaped like a fire hydrant. Perhaps a chair.

Monks stopped breathing. There were no chairs on the balcony.

He sat up. The shadow rose suddenly, too, expanding upward like a seal thrusting itself from the water.

He heaved himself across Alison, groping for his coat in the gloom, remembering in the same instant that he had locked the pistol in the Bronco—*Christ*. He lunged for the sliding door and threw his weight against it, fingers clawing to make sure it was latched. The shadow moved back.

He jerked the curtain open several inches, and stared at the frightened face of a teenaged boy, crouched with hands on the balcony railing, about to vault back over and once again flee.

Monks exhaled shakily. "It's Tanager."

He pulled the door open, wondering how the hell the boy had found them, then remembering her scribbled note. Alison stepped past him, wrapped in the bedspread. She hugged Tanager to her, pulling him inside.

"How'd you get here, Tanager?"

"Motorcycle."

"*Motorcycle?* My God, you must be freezing."

He had exchanged his shorts for long pants and put on a ski jacket, but they were soaked with rain. His face was milk white. She wrapped the bedspread around him and pressed him into a chair, then walked nude, with no trace of self-consciousness, to pick up her dress from the floor. Monks hastily pulled on his own clothes.

Tanager sat with hands clasped between his knees, thighs hugging his forearms, face turned aside, as if that way he could not really be seen. Alison knelt beside him, smoothing his hair like a mother or a nurse. In the quiet, Monks heard him swallow.

Alison said, "Why'd you get so scared?"

"She told me she was taking Caymas back to the hospital. Then you said he wasn't there."

"Who's *she?*"

"The other lady, who was here before you. Naia."

Tanager pronounced it to rhyme with *eye-uh*. Monks had never heard the name, or any cognate for the word. He glanced questioningly at Alison. She shook her head.

"Don't you know her?" Tanager said. "She knows you."

"Does she have another name?"

"That's all she told me."

Naia. A new player.

"Maybe I do know her," Alison said. "Maybe that's a nickname. Tell us what happened."

Monks listened silently, groping to interpret the boy's halting words.

Caymas had come home from Clevinger the previous fall. He quickly stopped taking his required medications, and instead was getting into the other kinds of drugs that pervaded the

area. He was irrational, aggressive, dangerous.
Far worse, it was clear that Alison had hit a nerve:
Tanager had been his brother's victim in the past,
and he was afraid it would start happening again.
He spent as much time as he could away from
home, especially at a deserted stretch of beach.

One afternoon he met a woman named Naia
walking there. She was hard for the boy to
describe: older than Alison, heavy makeup, slender, wearing a wide-brimmed hat and sunglasses.
At first, there was no clue that this was anything
but accident.

She asked him his age. He was almost sixteen.
What would he get for his birthday, if he could
have anything? A motorcycle that an older friend
wanted to sell.

Monks remembered the crotch-rocket shape,
carefully tarped beside the cabin: the bike Tanager had ridden here.

It was not hard to understand how desperate
that urge for freedom must have been.

Tanager's dream was an empty one: there was
no way he was going to put his hands on eighteen
hundred dollars. But Naia told him that she
worked for "the hospital." They wanted to take
Caymas back, but were afraid someone might get
hurt, like last time. They would be glad to pay
eighteen hundred dollars if Tanager would show
them Caymas's hideout back in the woods. That
way, they could wait for Caymas there and take
him back safely.

No one else would ever have to know about Tanager's part in it.

He sniffled in the silence. Alison stood and moved to stand behind him, her hands rubbing his shoulders. "What does everybody else think happened to Caymas?" she said.

"He's just gone."

"Maybe they took him to a different hospital," she said soothingly. "That could be what happened, Tanager."

"Caymas, he had this belt buckle." He blurted the words, as if he had been holding them back. "He showed it to me one night. He was laughing, doing crank. He said, 'You know what this is? Money.' He said, 'The bitch thought she was getting me to take somebody down. But she liked sucking on me so much, she forgot to be careful. I made her buckle me back up when she was done. Now I got her prints.'"

"Do you think that's who Caymas meant? Naia?"

"I don't know!"

"What happened then?" she said.

"Caymas got some money in the mail. I think it was a lot."

"And then Naia came?"

Nod.

"Do you know where the buckle is?"

"No. Caymas buried things."

Monks stepped to the sliding door and pushed it open. Cool misty air blew in, heavy with the smell of the sea. Beyond the rocky headland bluffs, he could see a fishing boat coming into Noyo Harbor, the channel lighted by buoys bobbing on the dark Pacific swells.

Caymas buried things. Like the body of a nine-year-old boy.

"Tanager," Alison said. "What did Naia say about me?"

"I found a note, day before yesterday. Taped to my handlebars."

"Do you have it?"

"I threw it away."

"But you remember what it said?"

" 'Take Alison where you took me. Tell her to look in the stovepipe.' "

"Will you take us there?"

"Am I going to have to talk to the police?"

She looked at Monks again. Her gaze warned him not to contradict her.

"You won't, Tanager," she said. "We promise."

In the parking lot, Monks watched the boy hurry off to his motorcycle.

An unidentified *she* had enlisted Caymas Schulte to "take somebody down," offering a sexual favor in the bargain. Whoever she was, she did not want her identity known. But Caymas had been cunning enough to get her fingerprints and blackmail her.

Soon after that, Naia showed up.

And Caymas disappeared.

It was hard to escape the conclusion that "she" was Naia, who had come to eliminate the threat of Caymas and the telltale belt buckle. But Tanager had been able to ignore cause and effect, convincing himself that Caymas had been taken away for everyone's good.

Until tonight. Now, every time he looked at that bike, he was going to think about how he got it.

Caymas Schulte's hideout was an abandoned logging camp. The long-disused roads that led to it were covered with redwood duff and brush, unrecognizable to anyone who did not know them. Tanager led the way on his motorcycle, Monks following cautiously in four-wheel drive, trying to keep the bike's taillight in view through the fog. He reckoned they had gone about two miles from the highway when Tanager stopped.

They went the final few hundred yards on foot, Monks lighting the way with a flashlight. Tanager was half-running now, in a hurry to get this over with. The camp was in a clearing on the bank of a stream. There were several ruined old wooden buildings, with one iron-roofed shed still standing.

Alison jerked at Monks's coat and mouthed the words in his ear: "That photo."

This was where the picture of Caymas had been snapped.

"In there," Tanager said, pointing to the shed. His voice was barely above a whisper. "I'm going now, okay?"

Alison turned toward him, but he was already skipping backwards, then gone in the fog.

The shed held a bunk with a tattered mattress and several shelves. A crude table had been built like a workbench under the single window. Monks walked across the wooden floor where a child had given up his life. His steps made a hollow sound.

Whatever stove might have been there was gone, but the pipe was still in the wall, filled with ashes and debris. He reached in, brushing them aside, and touched a smooth cool surface. Plastic.

It was a food container about the size of a shoebox. Monks lifted it out and set it on the table. He opened his pocketknife and gave it to Alison, then held the flashlight while she worked open the lid. The contents were wrapped in several layers of tissue, as the photo had been. Her fingers parted them to reveal a man's face.

It was chalk white, sculpted out of ceramic or clay, life-sized and extraordinarily lifelike. The nose was thick and the cheeks heavy, suggesting strength. But the impact was in the expression: desperation, pain, rage, forcibly captured. As the box turned in her hands, shadows played across the features, making them seem to move. Monks felt his scalp prickle.

Alison said, "Caymas."

She lifted the mask out delicately, as if it were a wounded bird. Beneath it in the box lay a second object: a red, much worn, 49ers baseball cap.

Monks glimpsed something quivering on the mask's back, like moonlit water.

He said, "Hold it up."

The something was a dark image of his own face, reflected in an oval mirror imbedded in the clay.

He moved beside her, so he was looking over her shoulder.

"Turn it around," he said.

As her face came full-sized in the mirror, he saw that two red circles had been painted onto its surface, so that her eyes appeared to be ringed in blood.

Monks said, "A death mask?" He steered carefully along the fogbound road, heading back toward the motel.

"They made them in older cultures. Pressed wet clay against the face, then used it as a mold."

"What's the message?"

"The mirror. Naia wants to tell me there's a bond between us."

"You're talking about someone who seems to have killed a very dangerous man."

Alison crossed her arms tightly. The plastic box rested between her feet on the Bronco's floor.

"This is about trust. Not trying to threaten me."

"It's about murder, Alison. We'll stop at the sheriff's on our way in."

"We promised Tanager he wouldn't have to talk to the police."

"*You* did," Monks said, and immediately regretted his tone. He recognized the too-familiar strain of adrenaline and fatigue. "Sorry to bark. This is no game."

"I know it's not a game, Rasp. I'm around violent men every day."

"You might see the potential. I see the results, in the ER."

"It's *my* ass on the line."

"What are you telling me?"

"I don't want to go to police yet. I think she's asking for help."

Monks stared at her. "Are we talking pity here, Alison? What about the kid? She could have found Caymas's place without using him. Now he has to live with selling Caymas out. There's a cruelty at work."

"Maybe she doesn't see it that way. Maybe she was giving him a chance to get even for what Caymas did to him. Means for him to be proud."

The rain had gotten heavier in Fort Bragg. The streets were deserted. Monks pulled into the motel parking lot.

He said, "It seems to me you're trying goddamned hard to put a pretty face on Naia."

She picked the box up from the floor and turned to face him.

"I started doing this work because I wanted to find out what makes people turn into monsters. But if you dig too deep there, the mainstream brands you as a freak. So I've been a good girl, played by the rules. And you know what I am? A prison guard, with Haldol for a gun."

She opened the door, moving away from him in a way he could feel.

"If this was a mistake," she said, and tossed her head in a gesture that included everything but centered on the bed in her room, "it was my mistake. I'll talk to you tomorrow."

Monks walked unhappily to his own room. When he called her twenty minutes later, she did not answer. The desk told him that she had checked out.

He packed and started his own long drive home.

10

The ring of her telephone brought Alison awake, fumbling to reach it. She was on her living room couch, still dressed, covered by a quilt. The clock read 3:53 A.M. She had gotten home from Mendocino less than an hour earlier, exhausted. The bedroom had seemed too far away.

She said, "Hello?"

For several seconds, there was no sound but faint static.

"Hello," she said again, annoyed now that it was probably a wrong number. "If you can hear me, I can't hear you." Her finger moved to click off the phone.

"It was awfully late at night to go bird watching." The voice was an eerie whisper: high-pitched, childlike.

"Bird watching?"

"You went looking for a woodbird?"

Woodbird. *Tanager*. She woke up fast, scanning the windows as if a face might be there.

"Who is this?"

"Did he sing for you?" the whisper asked.

"We—talked. Yes."

"I'm more and more impressed. At first I was afraid you'd be just another pretty face."

Alison tried for the same playful tone. "Where have we met?"

A hint of laughter. "Did he tell you my name?"

She said, "Naia?"

"Do you know what it means?"

"I'm afraid I don't."

"It's the genus name for cobras. Naia is the queen."

Alison said, "Cobras?"

"*You* know." The tone was a child's firm insistence.

She hesitated, off balance from the responses that did not seem to follow any logic.

"Do you have another name?"

"I'd like to start therapy with you," the voice said.

"I'd like that too."

"Don't. You. *Ever*. Condescend to me like one of your filthy patients."

The tone had changed instantly to cold fury. Alison swallowed, a dry, hard knotting of her throat.

"I'm sorry."

A pause. "Did you enjoy your gift?"

Her gaze moved to the plastic box on the coffee table.

"It's—disturbing."

The unseen tongue clucked mockingly. "You're shocked?"

"I can't condone murder."

"I think you're lying to yourself. Don't you sometimes tell your patients that?"

"I don't say it that way."

"Why don't you tell me what you really feel, instead of what you think you should?"

Alison lifted the lid off the box and gazed down at the chalk-white death mask of Caymas Schulte. She thought about the child he had murdered and buried, with no one knowing how many others he might have damaged. The terror in his own brother's face. The queasy sense she had felt in his presence, that some alien thing was hiding inside him, barely contained, waiting for its instant to leap out, rend, destroy, then disappear back until its next chance came.

She said, "I feel relief that he's gone."

"Is that all? A man you were terrified of? It thrills you. Admit it."

"I can't."

"He's yours now."

"What do you mean?"

The laughter again. "What else did the wood-bird tell you?"

Fear for the boy touched her. "He was very careful."

"But you weren't so careful. There was someone with you. A man." The tone was dangerously edged again.

She inhaled deeply and stared out the French doors as the implication hit. The lights of the San Francisco coastline shimmered through the rain, distant as stars.

She said, "I was afraid to go alone. You can understand that, can't you?"

"Is he someone special?"

Her mind moved swiftly, searching for the right course.

"He's not in this. He was just company."

"Tell me then," the voice said archly. "Did you fuck your company?"

Alison hesitated. "No."

"*No?* I can *smell* your lie, you slut." The voice ripped into her. Her teeth came together in a quick clattering.

"Yes," Alison said. "I did."

"What a generous girl." The voice was calm again, gently inquisitive. "Suck him?"

"Yes."

"Did he make you come?"

"Yes."

"How?"

"He knows what I like."

"I want to know, too."

"He went down on me. Then I was on top."

"Go on."

"I think—he hadn't had a woman in a while."

"Was he too quick?"

"Very hard."

"That pleases you?"

"Of course."

"Of course," the voice repeated musingly. "What will we do about him?"

"There's no need to do anything. I'll just tell him nothing more has happened. He'll go away."

"This is just between us, now. Yes?"

Alison said, "Yes."

Silence. Thirty seconds. Forty. Rain splattered the windows in a sudden hard gust.

"I'm not interested in birds," the voice said. "Let's talk about noble prey. Serpents. Considered by the ancients to be immortal, because they regenerate their skins. Symbols of wisdom and healing. The caduceus. And hermaphroditic, when depicted as circular, with the phallic tail penetrating the mouth. Have you ever seen a cobra? A live one?"

"I'm—not sure. Maybe when I was little, in a zoo."

"They're particularly splendid. Intelligent. But the deadliest species of cobra walks on two legs."

"Like Caymas?"

"Like him. Let's go for a stroll, shall we?"

"All right. Where?"

"A dark place. A lair, a den. Close your eyes."

Alison did.

"There's a dangerous creature loose," the voice said. "A cobra. Very vicious, very cunning. You have to be *more* dangerous. Faster, smarter. See in the night."

"I'm not strong like you are."

"No," the harsh voice said. "You're a little quail, mincing around the entrance. You peek in at the cobras to get your dreary, timid thrills. You tease them with a stick you hold in your little beak. But you've been oh, so careful."

Eyes still closed, Alison said, "What happens then? When you walk into that den?"

A high skittering laugh. "Oh, darling. Everything changes. You become a cobra *hunter*."

For an instant, she glimpsed again that dark inner landscape, with its searching presence that promised to reveal the longed-for mystery. Her senses returned slowly, as if she were reawakening. The room was warm, fragrant with the greenery of plants.

She said, "How can a quail hunt a cobra?"

"You already know. You just have to realize it. Hold your gift. Turn it over."

Alison gazed down into the mirror, into her own blood-ringed eyes at the someone she was supposed to be.

"Tell me who I'm looking at," she said.

"She got lost." The voice was smaller now,

subdued. "In a dark place, a cellar. A cobra found her."

"Were you there?"

"That's how Naia was born."

Alison stood and walked to the French doors, watching her reflection approach in the rain-streaked glass.

She said, "I've been waiting for you."

"You can use your gift."

"How?"

"The mask traps the escaping life force, dear. That's its purpose. The purest form of power."

"I don't understand."

"You will. Do you know what happens if you throw a piglet into a cage with two hungry cobras?"

"No."

"They start eating it from either end. Then one will swallow the other. That's what Naia does. She turns them on each other and harvests the victors."

Alison opened the French doors and stepped onto the deck. A hundred yards away, down the rocky slope, dark surf boomed and ebbed with a cold sucking sound.

"You're going to get *strong*," the voice said.

Alison said, "You haven't told me what I can give you. In return."

"The lost girl isn't really lost," the voice said softly. "She's coming home. Soon."

The phone clicked.

"Hello?" Alison said. "Can you still hear me?"

She stood clasping the mask of Caymas Schulte, her fingers moving over the cold pain-wracked features. Approving of him at last, for being dead.

11

Dr. Roman Kasmarek was a youthful forty-five, slender, dark, with wire-rimmed glasses and dabs of Vick's glistening under his nostrils. Monks found him preparing for his first autopsy of the day in Mercy Hospital's morgue, a windowless concrete room with drains set into the floors. One wall had a bank of what looked like giant filing cabinets, one of which might still contain Ismael Esposito.

Roman said, "Let me run this through once more. You want me to check surrounding counties for coroners' reports that may or may not exist, using hospital facilities, even though this is in no way related to hospital business, and not disclosing the true reason for the inquiries. All of which violates professional ethics in several ways that could have serious repercussions for, say, me."

"I didn't put it quite like that."

"Is this related to your investigation work, Carroll? Or just a new hobby?"

"I don't know what it is," Monks said, which, in the light of day, was becoming truer. "A friend, a psychologist, approached me."

Monks laid the printout of the four missing NGIs on a stainless steel dissecting table: Wayne Prokuta, Kenneth Foote, Brad Kurlin, and Caymas Schulte. Roman scanned the litanies of violence, drumming his fingers. The drumming slowed, then stopped.

They had first worked together more than a decade earlier at Bayview, when Monks was head of the ER and Roman, assistant pathologist. When the missing tape incident occurred, and Monks had been forced to divide the world between friends and others, Roman stood firm. A year later, he became chief pathologist at Mercy and Monks was unemployed. Among the first things Roman had done was to use his influence to bring Monks to Mercy's ER.

"All these men have disappeared after release," Monks said. "The follow-up's piss poor and there's reason to think at least one has been killed. I'm wondering if any have turned up in the morgues."

"Don't misunderstand me, it's not that I have any moral objections to lying. I'm just not good at it."

"The fewer people who know about this, the better, Roman. My friend was contacted by somebody who may be the killer."

Roman looked up owlishly.

"I assume that means you'd like these ASAP?"

"Sorry to be pushy."

"I have a backlog of patients, but none of them are urgent appointments. I can get anything in San Francisco and Marin. Maybe San Jose. Sacramento and Mendocino are long shots. I don't know the MEs in those areas."

Monks said, "There's one more. Robert Vandenard IV."

"Vandenard?"

"He was the heir. Committed suicide in '87 or '88. The body was found near Napa."

"Carroll. Asking about these other guys is one thing. With a name like Vandenard, people might want to know why."

"It could be the most important one."

"I'll think of something," Roman said. "Why don't you check back about noon."

The medical records building at Clevinger Hospital was gray and uninviting. Alison had only been inside a few times. Files for current patients were kept on-ward, with aides transferring them as needed.

Posters in English and Spanish—NOTICE! AVISO!—papered the lobby walls, proclaiming information everyone either already knew or cared nothing about. The chipped Formica counter was an uncomfortable orange color that reminded her of Dreamsicles she had eaten as a kid.

The clerk, a sinewy black woman with a long slender neck, ignored her for the requisite minute or so. Finally she looked up from her computer monitor, busy fingers pausing. Her name tag read Ms. Willis.

"I need access to Dr. Jephson's audit," Alison said. "I work for him." She held up her ID card.

"You new here, miss?"

"No."

"Uh-huh. Cause unless you're authorized, there's a procedure. You fill out a form—" a brilliant red-tipped fingernail jabbed at a stack of papers in a plastic stand "—and leave it there." The finger sliced through the air to another untidy pile of perhaps twenty, waiting to be collected. "You come pick up the files when they're ready. We'll call you." She swiveled back to her computer, as if to avenge the waste of her time.

"I'm sorry, but it has to be now."

"You and everybody else." The red-tipped fingers danced across the keyboard.

"I'm trying to save you trouble. I can work here, I don't need to take them out."

Ms. Willis exhaled. "How many files?"

"Sixty-eight."

She sank back in her chair. "Honey, you have got to be kidding."

"I wish I was."

She stood, came to the counter and examined Alison's ID.

"You're on Three-Psych, huh?"

"Yes."

"How long you want here?"

"Two hours?"

"You're going to do sixty-eight files in two hours? I thought it's the patients supposed to be crazy over there." She sniffed in exasperation. "Come on."

Lugging briefcase and purse, Allison followed Ms. Willis through the racks into the hospital's memory. They passed a few others, pallid shapes moving like spectral souls in a purgatory of weary search for information, endlessly removing and replacing files for their own obscure purposes. Which included the illegal sale of confidential material, such as bungled medical procedures, to lawyers, who would then contact the victims to instigate malpractice suits.

She settled her things in a carel, then stood before the section of shelves marked DR. JEPHSON AUDIT. It was several feet wide and reached from her waist to above her head: the files of sixty-eight NGIs, killers, rapists, child molesters, men like John James Garlick who were murderous bombs primed to go off at the next chance. Some of the files were inches thick.

If Naia was a released NGI, it was just possible

that somewhere, in one of them, there would be a hint: mention of a lost girl. Of belated mastery: a trauma victim seeking to relive the experience again and again, until he or she felt control had been gained. Of cobras—which, the dictionary had confirmed, were of the genus *Naia*.

Alison scanned as fast as she could, skipping the thousands of pages of medical records and psychiatric evaluations, concentrating on criminal histories and interviews—especially interviews with Dr. Francis Jephson, who was emerging in her mind as the primary candidate for Naia.

The man she had been working for, harboring this secret. Someplace short of outright psychosis, a no man's land of compartmentalization: one aspect moral, the other deadly, and the two able to exist side by side without apparent conflict. Last night's conversation couched in symbols, hiding behind another form of mask. The den, a secret storehouse of violence. The lost girl, innocence or restraint. Naia, the cobra, the personality that acted out. Underneath a placid exterior life, the intense superiority of being the only one who knew the truth.

Perhaps even a darker heart: the savage thrill of releasing killers among the unsuspecting—and then killing the killers.

She turns them on each other and harvests the victors.

Her search turned up nothing. Except that

toward the end, head aching from small print and fluorescent lights, she discovered that the file of one Thomas David Springkell, released 3/14/88, was missing.

Stover Larrabee sipped black coffee, grimacing. They were at a Zim's on Nineteenth Avenue, an old-fashioned diner busy with customers who looked like they spent a lot of time there. It was a few minutes before 10 A.M.

Monks said, "Sorry to get you up so early."

"I'll get over it. Naia, huh?" Monks detected a note of admiration. "Sounds like she ought to be on the SFPD payroll."

"Smart enough to set up a man like Caymas Schulte," Monks said. "Strong enough to take him out. God knows what else."

"What seems clear is that Dr. Chapley has attracted the attention of a highly dangerous individual. She should leave the area immediately. Contact the FBI. Consider assuming a new identity until Naia is apprehended."

"She's unwilling to do that. She's convinced she's not in danger, that there's a trust being extended. If she violates it, that might anger Naia. I've thought about approaching the police on my own."

"Except she might be right?"

Monks exhaled. "It's not my decision to make. Yet."

Larrabee said, "Have you considered the possibility that Dr. Chapley is somehow involved in this?"

"She likes to play games, Stover. I can't believe she'd pull something that would scare a teenage kid. But I can sure believe she'd flirt with trouble, past the point of sense."

Monks studied the several photos of Francis Jephson that Larrabee had downloaded from computer sources. He was built slightly, with a fine-boned handsome face: a distance runner, Alison had said.

"You think Naia could be a man? Jephson, cross-dressing?"

"He might have fooled a kid like Tanager," Monks said. "It's tougher to believe he could give a blow job to somebody he'd been doing therapy with and not have the guy recognize him."

"Not that tough."

Monks smiled. "What do you think about having him picked up?"

"What you've got on him now isn't going to keep him in jail. It *would* wave a red flag. Put Dr. Chapley right where she's afraid of being."

Monks said, "What do you suggest?"

"Keep gathering information and try to get something solid linking Jephson to a murder. If it doesn't happen quick, I think Dr. Chapley's going to have to go into hiding, whether she wants to or not." Larrabee finished his coffee and stood. "We've got two hours. Wonder what Bernard Capaldi's doing this morning?"

Bernard Capaldi: friend and attorney to the Vandenards. Almost certainly the man who had arranged for Robby literally to get away with murder once. Maybe twice.

"Dennis seemed to think he was dying," Monks said.

"He might have us thrown down the stairs. On the other hand, there's nothing like a ticking clock to make a guilty man talkative."

As they walked to the car, Larrabee said, "You ever been around that? Somebody who comes across as normal, and then in an eyeblink turns into a batshit killer?"

"Plenty of marines."

"If we do meet Naia and you figure it out, try not to let her know it," Larrabee said. "Although she will."

The man who answered the door at Bernard Capaldi's Pacific Heights home looked more like an ex-boxer than a butler. Monks and Larrabee waited in a tiled foyer while he stepped into a side room to announce the visitors. The room's partially open door gave a glimpse of video monitors from surveillance cameras around the property.

He came back out and faced them, neither polite nor rude. "Mr. Capaldi will be down in a few minutes. You gentlemen care for something to drink?"

They declined. He led them into a drawing room with ocean-facing windows that reached from the floor almost to the twelve-foot ceiling, and a central curving staircase with ornate balustrades. A Steinway grand piano occupied one corner. The woodwork glowed with the sheen of generations of care.

Monks had seen photographs of Bernard Capaldi in his glory days. He was a commanding presence, tall and spare, with the arched nose and ascetic features of a Renaissance-era Italian cardinal.

It was the same man who came toward them now, pushed in a wheelchair by a pretty nurse, but he had shrunken into himself. His face was gaunt, his hair a silver mist, and his skin had a yellowish waxy quality that Monks recognized, of someone nearing death. But the presence remained.

Capaldi smiled faintly. "A physician and a private detective. I think I can assume this is not a social call." He patted the nurse's hand. She tucked the blanket around his lap and left.

"Mr. Capaldi," Larrabee said. "We know you don't need to cooperate with us. But we believe there's a tangible danger to our client."

"Are you Larrabee?"

"Yes, sir."

"The Larrabee who shot that Fisherman's Wharf mugger, back—when was it, '86?"

"Yeah."

Monks turned to him, astonished. He had not known.

Capaldi said, "And got suspended?"

Larrabee nodded, tightlipped.

"Is that why you left the police force?"

"It figured in."

"Not very fond of lawyers, I'd guess?"

"Some more than others."

Capaldi laughed, a ghostly hacking sound. "Are you taping this?"

"No."

"I hardly need to point out that it would be a waste of time to try to depose me."

Monks said, "Osteosarcoma?"

Capaldi's gaze sharpened. "Correct."

"I'm told it's hellish."

"If you can imagine having your bones chewed out from the inside."

"I'm sorry," Monks said, feeling the inadequacy of the words.

"I'm eighty-four, Doctor. I have no complaints. But I tire quickly." His eyebrows rose in query.

Larrabee said, "We're representing a client who's looking into the past of Dr. Francis Jephson."

"Jephson," Capaldi said musingly. "Haven't heard that name in years."

"It's come clear that Robby Vandenard was in a position to compromise Jephson. Ruin him, even send him to prison. Was there any suspicion that Robby was murdered?"

Capaldi considered for half a minute.

"The answer is no, there was no such suspicion. A shotgun that had belonged to his father was still in his hand."

Monks recalled the deserted Napa mansion, with its neglected vineyards and the ominous doors closing off the site of Katherine Vandenard's murder. And nearby, the place Robby had chosen to take his own life.

"Would we be justified in suspecting that strings were pulled in getting Robby into Jephson's program at Clevinger Hospital?"

He deliberated again. "I'll allow your suspicion to rest unchallenged."

"Do you think Robby killed his sister?"

"Yes."

Larrabee turned away, hand going to his hair.

"Are you shocked, Mr. Larrabee? The rights and wrongs of it were cloudy. It was not a crime of hatred: the opposite. Robby knew what he was, early on in his life. Knew the world would see him as ugly and twisted. He saw Katherine as his other half. Beautiful, desirable. But she grew up ahead of him and began to reject him. The pivotal incident seemed to be that he spied on her having sex with a boyfriend. It came home to him that he was losing her, and that, he could not bear."

"So you hired Jephson to cover for him."

"Again, it wasn't that simple. I was loyal to the family. I acted in what I believed to be their best interests. There seemed no point in destroying another child's life. But by the time it was all over—" Capaldi waved a hand in eloquent weariness. "I regretted bitterly the part I'd played."

Monks said, "What made you choose Jephson? He must have been just out of residency."

"I didn't choose him. Robby did. He had seen several other psychiatrists in the years before Katherine's death. Hadn't gotten along with any of them. But there was a chemistry between him and Jephson. Robby would ask to see him. They'd go for walks together. When the murder occurred, he was the obvious choice."

"Did it ever occur to you that Jephson might have condoned it? Even planted the idea?"

Capaldi was silent. His gaze appeared to be fixed on the windows. Finally he said, "That's territory I don't dare enter."

"And yet you hired him again, when Robby killed Merle Lutey."

Capaldi turned back to them, looking frailer. "Gentlemen, I'm afraid I'm wearing out."

"Mr. Capaldi, does the name Naia mean anything to you?"

"No."

A thin finger pressed a button on the wheelchair. The nurse walked briskly back into the room. As she wheeled him away, he waved an impatient hand at their murmured thanks.

"The guy was a vicious fuck," Larrabee said. "Pistol-whipping women *after* he got their purses. That kind of shit." He gunned his Taurus through a yellow light on Geary, heading back toward Mercy Hospital. "It was night. I chased him three blocks. The cocksucker got rid of his gun somehow, it was never found. The defense established reasonable doubt that he was the same guy."

"Kill him?"

"I wish to Christ I had. Blew out his spleen. The city paid all his medical bills, gave him a fat settlement, and suspended me."

"Did they ever convict him?"

"Nope. But the muggings stopped."

Monks and Larrabee followed Roman Kasmarek into his glassed-in office in the morgue.

"San Jose and Mendocino were busts," Roman said. "No reports on Kenneth Foote or Caymas Schulte. I've got a call into Napa for Vandenard."

Monks said, "Capaldi seemed convinced that Robby was a clear-cut suicide."

"Capaldi's been wiping those people's asses for fifty years," Larrabee said. "Let's see what Dr. Kasmarek has to say."

"I got luckier close to home," Roman said. "Walter Bruggeman, in Marin, remembered the Brad Kurlin case quite well. He died in a fire, apparently one he set."

Brad Kurlin, known killer of six by arson. Released as rehabilitated by Dr. Francis Jephson.

"There were a couple of things Walter wasn't

entirely comfortable with. But nobody wanted to take it any further, even the family."

"Things such as?"

"The body was badly charred. But the way Kurlin had fallen, the right side was more protected. There were bits of a foreign substance in the heel of that hand: DE, diatomaceous earth. It's composed largely of tiny shell fragments, so it survived the fire.

"In itself, the DE's not much help. It's widely used, industrial filters, swimming pools, things like that. Kurlin could have picked it up anywhere. It would have to have been imbedded forcefully—say, he slipped and fell.

"But there was another thing that didn't make it onto the report. A possibility that the tendons behind the right knee were severed."

Monks said slowly, "You're suggesting he'd been hamstrung?"

"To cut those tendons accidentally, you'd have to be thrashing around pretty hard. Of course if you're being burned alive, you probably are. The off-the-record take was, the fire moved a lot faster than he thought. It blocked whatever exit he'd figured on. He tried to kick out a window, the flames exploded, he tore himself up on the glass. Fell back inside and smoke got him."

"Does that work for you?"

Roman shrugged. "The ME's job is to establish a cause of death. From there it's up to law enforcement to worry about the why's.

"But this gets more interesting. I hit the long shot. Prokuta." Roman spread out a faxed document, from the coroner's office of Solano County.

They leaned over the report: dated 4/9/91, for Wayne Prokuta, bludgeoner of an elderly woman. Spring floods had washed up his body in the morass-like delta of the Sacramento River, into which he had presumably thrown himself several months earlier. The cause of death was listed as suicide by drowning. Prokuta had still been wearing the remnants of a coat with heavy barbell weights in the pockets.

Roman turned to the second page. It began with the heading EXTERNAL EXAMINA- TION: *The body is that of a white male, appearing approximately the stated age. Tissue decomposition and skin slipping are extremely advanced, and skeletal disarray has occurred from fish and animal predation.*

Roman's finger moved down the page. *Small amounts of a nonlocal substance identified as diatomaceous earth were found imbedded in the tissue of the right shin and knee . . .*

Monks said, "That DE again. I'd say our margins for suicide are getting slimmer."

"There's more yet."

Roman remained silent for another half minute, as if still considering stepping back. Then he turned the page and his forefinger moved to the beginning of a paragraph: *The right arm shows severe animal damage, with distress evident in the wrist joint and a spiral fracture in the upper humerus.*

"There are a lot of possibilities," Roman said. "Maybe he jumped from a cliff or bridge, and hit something. Maybe got chewed up by a coyote or cougar.

"Except animal jaws or impact don't typically produce spiral fractures. They come from torsion. Something twisting the arm until it breaks."

Alison answered her office phone. It was Monks, calling from Mercy Hospital.

"I had our pathologist find autopsy reports on two more of your NGIs, Prokuta and Kurlin," he said. "The first was made to look like a suicide, the other an accident. They may have been disabled someplace first, then dumped."

She closed her eyes. "Disabled?"

"Possibly hamstrung. Tendons behind the knee severed. Both had a substance known as diatomaceous earth imbedded in tissue. As if they'd been at the same place and fallen hard, or crawled."

What will we do about him?

I'll just tell him nothing more has happened. He'll go away.

This is just between us now. Yes?

Yes.

She said, "Look. I've gotten you into something that's none of your doing."

"That's not an issue, Alison. Your safety is."

"Rasp, there's *no reason* to think she's going to come after me. I'm not even sure I want to stop her."

"What are you saying?"

"Look who she's killing."

Monks said, "So now you're judge and jury?"

"I don't know what I am. There's something you could do that might help. If you still want to."

"You know I do."

"There's an NGI file missing from Records. It's the only one out of sixty-eight, and he overlapped with Robby Vandenard. Can you check him out?"

"Give me the name."

"Thomas David Springkell." She spelled it aloud. "Try to find out what he looks like. His size. If he could be the one Tanager saw."

Monks said, "When can I meet you?"

"I could stop in Berkeley on my way home," she said, "Sproul Plaza, call it five."

She hung up and sat another minute, looking inward, trying to get a glimpse of what direction to take.

You're a little quail, mincing around the den's entrance. You peek in at the cobras to get your dreary, timid thrills. You tease them with a stick you hold in your little beak. But you've been oh, so careful.

What happens then? When you walk into that den?

Oh, darling. Everything changes. You become a cobra hunter.

Mrs. R answered the phone in Jephson's office.

Alison said, "Paula, I really need to talk to Dr. Jephson. Could he find a couple of minutes for me?"

"If you'll just hold on, I'll ask." Mrs. R's tone was cool and brisk. Clearly, she had not forgotten their last exchange.

Thirty seconds later she came back on. "I'm sorry, Alison. He's very busy these next couple of days. Why don't you try again next week?"

Alison unlocked a desk drawer filled with weapons confiscated from patients over the years: penknives, Afro combs, taped razor blades. She touched several with her forefinger, prodding them as if they could move.

Yes, it was toying with a deadly snake. An attempt to flush it out of its den, by using another snake: John James Garlick.

It came to her that this was what a killer felt, the unreality of each irreversible step toward a line that could never be uncrossed. The model that experts agreed on: a thrill greater than any other, absolute power over a victim. The need growing to have it again and again, each time more refined and controlled, more fully savored.

In her notebook she made a rough sketch of Jephson's face, then drew it twice more with increasing accuracy. On the last one, she dark-

ened his glasses to sunglasses and fluffed the hair
out into a wig, accentuating the fine bone structure of his cheeks and jaw. The result was femi-
nine, attractive.

She put away the notebook and went on-ward,
to finish out the next hours as if nothing was
amiss.

12

Monks got out of the Bronco and joined Larrabee on the sidewalk in front of Thomas Springkell's last known address: his parents' home, near Crockett, on the south shore of Carquinez Straits. The street was wistfully named Linda Vista. The view was of the great muddy mouth of the Sacramento River, with a long-disused derrick anchored offshore and several retired ships of the navy's mothball fleet waiting for orders to the scrap yard.

Larrabee held up his PI license to the woman who half-opened the door.

"Is this about Tommy?" she said.

"Yes, ma'am." Larrabee added quickly, "He's not in any trouble."

"He doesn't live here anymore."

"We're not police, Mrs. Springkell," Larrabee said, and repeated emphatically, "Tommy's not in any trouble."

She pushed the door the rest of the way open and stepped back. The living room was small, the ceiling low, with the kind of heavy texture found in motels. The smell of cigarette smoke was strong. Phyllis Springkell was in her mid-fifties, with olive skin, dyed black hair, and a patient air that Monks was starting to recognize, of people who were familiar with visits from authorities.

She said, "I haven't heard from him in nine years. That's the truth."

"Any idea where he is?"

"No, but I know what he is. He's dead."

Monks turned away, folding his arms.

Larrabee said, "Do you have a reason for thinking that?"

"I'm his mother," she said, as if that explained everything, and perhaps, Monks thought, it did.

A criminal history of Thomas Springkell had showed him to be, in Larrabee's words, a punk. By his early twenties, he had accumulated almost thirty arrests, with numerous periods of confinement in youth facilities, jails, and mental institutions. His crimes mainly involved drug use and larceny that had evolved from petty theft to armed robbery. But offenses had turned up that were dated after his release from Clevinger in March 1988.

Presumably, another success for Francis Jephson.

"Mrs. Springkell, I realize this is painful, and I'm very sorry to put you through it," Larrabee said.

"You going to tell me what it's about?"

"All right, I'll be very straight with you. I've been hired by the defense in a drug case. A fairly major dealer. Your son's name came up. It's my job, it's standard practice, to find out if his testimony might be damaging to my client."

"He's dead," she said again. "He'd never go this long without being in touch." She sat heavily on the couch and reached for a pack of cigarettes.

Larrabee said, "You last saw him nine years ago?"

"Here. He'd moved back home, was living in his old room."

"This was after he got out of Clevinger Hospital?"

She nodded. "One afternoon he said he was going to see somebody about a job. His father'd been after him about it, trying to keep him busy. Build up his self-respect. He'd had a bunch of loser friends. Doing cocaine, freebase. We were afraid, if he started up with them again, he'd be gone for good.

"Tommy walked up to the shopping center, over the hill." She gestured the direction with her head. "He never came home."

"You don't feel there's any chance he might have just taken off? Be out there somewhere, too shy, or whatever, to call his mom?"

She shook her head.

"Any chance Tommy would have been in contact with Mr. Springkell?"

"You can ask him, if you want to go to Kuwait."

"Kuwait?"

"He's over there helping them rebuild. He worked in the shipyards at Mare Island until they closed."

"How long's he been in Kuwait?"

"Him and his new wife? Just about five years."

"How about Tommy's brothers and sisters?"

"If they heard anything about him, they'd tell me."

Monks saw a chance to express kinship, perhaps ease the tension.

"I spent a long year at Mare Island," he said.

"No kidding. In the yards?"

"In the navy."

"You a private eye too?"

"A physician," Monks said.

"No kidding. How are you in on this?"

"There are some medical aspects. Technical points."

She leaned back, crossed her legs, blew smoke in their direction. Her gaze had gone appraising.

Larrabee cleared his throat. "Mrs. Springkell, how did Tommy get chosen for the Clevinger program? My understanding is, it's usually for very violent men."

"After his last arrest, they did a psychiatric evaluation."

"Who did?" Monks said. "Dr. Jephson?"

She tilted her head toward Monks. "You know him?"

"No. Not really."

"He's a great man," she said fervently. "He figured out what nobody had before. Tommy was bipolar, what they used to call manic-depressive. Now they've got names for all that, ways to treat it. Back then, he was just a kid who got in trouble. He got branded at school, he couldn't do anything right. So of course, he didn't want to go."

"Did Tommy ever commit any violent crimes?"

"Never," she said, eyes and voice gone hard. "A few robberies."

Quite a few, Monks thought, some of them armed.

He said, "So Dr. Jephson chose Tommy, personally?"

"He even arranged the funding. We could never have afforded it."

"Did Dr. Jephson ever contact Tommy after he was released?"

"Not that I know of."

"How about Robert Vandenard, Mrs. Springkell? Did Tommy ever talk about him?"

"Richie Rich?" She stubbed out the cigarette.

Monks said, "Were they friends?"

"That's what Tommy thought. Robby told him they were going to live together after they got out. Be bachelor pals. Of course it didn't happen.

Tommy'd try to call him, but they'd always say he was out. Tommy got very depressed."

Monks said, "Do you have a photo of Tommy?"

They followed her down a narrow, dim hallway to a small room, a kid's room, a room it was hard to imagine could hold enough self-respect to help a twenty-seven-year-old man, back from half a dozen jails and mental hospitals. A cheap acoustic guitar leaned in one corner. The walls were hung with clashing posters: Joe Montana fading back to pass, Jerry Garcia in vivid psychedelic coloring. With abrupt, bittersweet shock he recalled the rooms of Tanager Schulte and of his own children, similarly decorated, with icons of their heroes.

"This is Tommy," Mrs. Springkell said. "With his brothers." Her finger touched a photo on the dresser, a wiry dark-haired boy in his early teens, who appeared to be the youngest of three. She touched another, a portrait. He was older, nice looking, with carefully combed hair and awkward smile. "High school. He didn't finish."

Monks said, "About how tall was, is, he, Mrs. Springkell?"

She glanced at him. "Five nine. Why?"

"Slender? I mean, he didn't gain a lot of weight when he got older." She was looking at him steadily now. It was a very direct gaze. "The way some people do," Monks finished lamely.

"No," she said. "He came home from the hospital way thin. I was feeding him all he'd eat. You trying to match him up to something?"

"I'm just trying to form a picture of him. I've got kids myself."

"Yeah?" she said, her tone caustic. "Do doctors' kids get in trouble?"

Monks said, "One has."

Larrabee said. "I hate to ask you this, Mrs. Springkell, but did Tommy ever exhibit any, uh, gay behavior? Anything like that?"

"What the hell has that got to do with a drug bust?"

Larrabee's hand went to his hair, brushing several times in boyish chagrin. "It's complicated."

"No. He liked girls but he never had much luck. That was another way the Vandenard kid let him down. He told Tommy he'd get them both girlfriends, then they could trade off with each other's in the dark, the girls would never know. Tommy took him seriously."

They followed her back to the living room. She went into the kitchen and opened a cabinet above a counter, displaying a selection of grocery store liquor in plastic bottles.

"The sun just went over the yardarm. That's what they say in the navy, isn't it?"

Monks said, "On certain occasions. Yes."

"You boys care to join me?" She looked directly at Monks. "We could talk about trouble."

Larrabee said, "We'd love to, but this case is coming up fast. We've still got calls to make. Mrs.

Springkell, you've been a terrific help. We may
be back."

"Is this really about a drug case?"

Larrabee said, "No."

"You'll let me know if you find out anything
about Tommy?"

"Yes, ma'am, we surely will."

Monks drove behind Larrabee down the
switchback road toward the river. They pulled
over at a vacant patch of ground and leaned on
the Bronco's hood, partly shielded from the wet
cutting wind off the water.

"You're the pro," Monks said. "Was she telling
the truth?"

"Mostly. It doesn't mean Tommy was straight
with her. Even that he's not still alive."

"There's nothing to suggest him as anything
like Naia. He'd have to have undergone a complete personality change."

Larrabee grunted. "Not to mention smarten-
ing up. What I'm starting to wonder is, could
Naia be two people? Say Jephson got his hooks
into Tommy. Brainwashed him. He calls the
shots, Tommy does the legwork."

"I think that's mostly in the movies, Stover,"
Monks said, but found himself reconsidering. Jephson was a specialist in behavior modification. There
was no telling how far an already unstable mind
could be pushed by a skilled practitioner, especially
one with access to a wide variety of psychotropic
drugs and no scruples about using them.

"It is a hell of a coincidence, Tommy and Robby Vandenard being in there together, and then that file turning up missing," he said. As if Jephson had known that it obtained something damaging to him, and destroyed it.

"Why else would Jephson go to such trouble to get Tommy into the program, even pay his way?" Larrabee said. "No money in it. No prestige in rehabbing a punk. He had a use for him."

"Like getting rid of Robby?"

"That's running through my mind. Say he encouraged their friendship, knowing that Robby would break it off. Then worked on Tommy to get even with the pal who fucked him over."

"You think a Thomas Springkell could overpower a Caymas Schulte?" Monks said.

"I think you could take out just about anybody if you got the drop on them. But to hamstring these guys, break their bones, dump them, without a whisper of suspicion. Christ knows how many times, over a period of years."

Larrabee turned his back to the wind and shoved his hands in his pockets.

"I'm plenty impressed by Naia. But I'm not real interested in getting to know her better."

Four P.M. was a quiet time on Three-Psych, meds at the peak of their effect, staff staying scarce and coasting. Alison stepped out of her office. In the pocket of her skirt she carried a flesh-pink toothbrush that had been sharpened to a point by rubbing against concrete.

John James Garlick was in his usual place at the courtyard's far end, hands in pockets, leaning against the fence. The pose was youthful, even appealing, and the thought came to her: *a predator's natural camouflage*.

Soon to be released.

She stepped into sight in the doorway. The NGIs turned quickly, keen to notice entrances and exits. A few of them murmured greetings before turning away in disinterest or unease. Her gaze remained on Garlick until he looked again. She mouthed his name and gestured invitingly, by the book, as nonthreatening as possible. He approached slowly.

"I wondered if we could talk a minute, John. About your post-release plans." She could feel the eyes measuring her from behind the polite veil: the look of an experienced con, concerned only with what he stood to gain or lose. He was clear, controlled, and in that moment she was certain that he had not been taking his meds.

She started to walk back into the building. "Dr. Jephson feels your therapy's been a great success."

For a heartbeat longer, she felt the measuring intensify. Then he grinned, a quick flash of clean teeth that something even in her responded to, and she had to fight the urge to swallow. It was as if an evil secret had been revealed: this was how he had done it, the contrition and impish smile, the glib salesman's tongue, the bad boy who mom would always forgive one more time. A pattern which might have continued lifelong, if he had not finally pushed past the point where even the most tearful remorse was of no avail.

"I'll never forget the people who straightened me out," he said.

"You're going live at home? Work for your father?"

"My move is to take things slow. Right?"

"Exactly right," she said. She stepped out into the garden, meagerly tended by patients, with not much remaining of the summer's efforts but a few straggling rows of corn. It was never crowded and sure to be deserted at a time like this.

"You're feeling confident about the adjustment?"

"I don't see I have anything to be worried about, Doctor. I made mistakes, but that's all done with."

"I assume Dr. Jephson has arranged for you to keep in touch?"

His eyes widened in a quick, mock innocent flash. "Why? You want to get together?"

She smiled and kept moving, slow pacing that took them farther into the garden.

"Just in case you did feel trouble coming on. He's told you to call him first, hasn't he?"

The wary look slid across Garlick's eyes like a reptile's membranes.

"Nobody else will know," she said. "Is that what he told you?"

He looked past her toward the door. "What's this to you?"

"Professional interest."

He grimaced contemptuously and side-stepped, but she moved to block him.

"When did you stop taking your meds, John?"

"I take meds three times a day, lady."

"You realize I'm not going to be able to recommend your release."

That something *other* beyond human or animal flared in his eyes, its force and suddenness stopping her breath. Slowly, the rage receded, veneered over by thin tight control.

"You don't have any fucking thing to do with it," Garlick said.

"I have everything to do with it. Answer me. Did Dr. Jephson offer to keep in touch with you privately?"

Very quietly, Garlick said, "When I'm released, I'll report once a month to the outpatient clinic in Santa Rosa for decanoate treatment. Okay? Now I'd like to leave."

"Did he ever come on to you sexually, John? Is that what you're so angry about?"

"Out of my fucking *way*."

Her hand gripped the makeshift weapon in her pocket.

"Did he ever use the name Naia?"

The look was back in his eyes again, at the breaking point, the last instant to back off. She stared into the bristling menace that had killed one woman and injured several more, and raised the toothbrush into his view.

"You know what this is?" she said. "Your ticket back to Atascadero. For assaulting me, right here, right now. Your word against mine."

His movement was like the strike of a snake, slapping the toothbrush down. His other hand went to her neck, fingers gripping the collar of her blouse, ripping it halfway open as she pulled away. He glided after her, crouched, simian, and she saw with disbelief the erection bulging the thin fabric of his scrubs. Those eyes from another world burned into her, his peeled back lips crooning the words:

"Ohh, I can just hear the *sounds* you're gonna make."

His fist shot toward her in a blur, knuckles catching the edge of her jaw and bringing a silent painless explosion in her brain. His fingers tore into her hair and incredible strength forced her to her knees, dragging her, with his voice panting sounds that might have been words. She twisted, fighting, flailing her arms behind. He wrenched her head back, poised to ram it into the raw concrete of the wall.

In that instant she became aware of another noise blasting her senses: the half-second bursts of the assault alert, filling the building.

Then Harold Henley was there, his blue-shirted body the size of an upended wheelbarrow.

"You get hold yourself, Mister Garlick," Harold said with venomous calm. "You try real hard." The rest of the assault team was arriving now, in a group as if they had been somewhere hiding: attendants and aides, another PSO, the pair of gay psych techs known as Tom and Jerry, carrying a restraint belt. Garlick stayed rigid, hand twisted in her hair as if it were the mane of a rebellious horse, holding her tight against his legs.

"Let her go, Garlick," Harold said, and Garlick did, shoving her head forward. Harold stepped to her and pulled her to her feet. She stumbled to safety. Garlick was backing away, fingers rigid, lips skinned back to bare his teeth. The assault team was in action now, circling him. Jerry dropped to hands and knees behind him, the prop over which Garlick would be pushed and tripped.

But Garlick had been through this before and he was waiting for it. He whirled and brought his foot up with vicious fury into the tech's outstretched abdomen. The sound was something she could feel. Garlick was fast enough to get a knee to Jerry's face before Harold piled into him. The others grabbed for his flailing limbs and the group went down, gasping and cursing. One wiry leg was still free, lashing like a calf's in a branding chute. Alison fell on it, taking a knee to the chest with stunning force, hugging it with her face pressed against the sour-smelling scrubs while his kicks slid her back and forth like a dustmop.

Tense hands pressed the snarling face down hard, distorting his flesh, and snaked the restraint belt around his waist inches at a time. At last it was secure, his wrists manacled, and Harold knelt beside her to grip the ankle she held. He locked the cuffs on, and she rolled away and lay with her eyes closed, fighting nausea.

Someone gripped her arms and helped her stand. She steadied her breathing, holding the torn blouse together at her throat. Jerry was sitting pale and bloody-faced while his partner examined him tenderly. The aides had brought a gurney and were cautiously strapping Garlick onto it, while he snarled a litany of threat. The charge nurse, Mrs. Guymon, had come from the Nurses' Station and waited inquiringly. Everybody knew the drill but it had to be official.

Alison said, "Five milligrams of droperidol, IM. Get Dr. Ghose to sign it off."

The aides wheeled Garlick past. His eyes locked with hers again, and she understood that never, for the rest of his life, would he forget being forced to surrender to her.

Harold stood beside her, watching. His face, in profile, was grim.

"That was fast," she said. "Thanks."

"She make the punishment fit the crime."

Alison stared at Harold in astonishment, not sure she had heard right, but he was already following the gurney to Seclusion. "You should see someone," Mrs. Guymon said to Alison. Both knew that it was not physical damage she was talking about.

"I'm all right. There'll need to be an assault team meeting." This was another form of therapy, for the keepers: debriefing sessions designed to dissipate the fear and rage that might otherwise lead to time-honored forms of staff retaliation, beatings, starvation, psychosis-inducing medication overdoses, even hacked genitals.

Mrs. Guymon left, too. The toothbrush was lying against the wall. Allison pocketed it unseen and walked to her office past a collage of patients' stares, fearful, childlike, blank.

Inside, she raised her fingers to explore the tenderness of her face and neck.

But her fear vanished in sudden elation.

You become a cobra hunter.

There was not going to be any early release for John James Garlick now.

She shrugged on her raincoat, buttoning it to the neck, and gathered her things. Harold was waiting at the main door.

She said, "What did you mean earlier about the punishment fitting the crime?"

"Alison." He glanced up and down the hall.

No one stood near. His face tightened into the expression of a concerned adult trying to explain a difficult concept to a child.

"They a *world* out there. You come in here, you think you seeing that world, but you only seeing a little part of it."

The door closed behind her with a cold metallic clang.

She walked to her car, quickly at first, then slowing down. She had left it unlocked.

But today, there was no gift.

Monks waited at Sproul Plaza, where Telegraph Avenue met the Berkeley campus: nursery of the sixties, where the SDS had preached a revolution that never came, where crowds had gathered to demonstrate, battle police, and put an end to a faraway war. He had first visited here on his way to that same war, feeling, with his short hair and civvies, like a sacrificial animal among pagans. Now most of the students looked more like he had then, clean-cut frat types or career-seekers. But Telegraph seemed unchanged, with its sidewalk stalls of jewelry merchants, the same outfits and long hair.

A group of skateboarders bullied their way through the crowd: aggressive, energetic, a little frightening. These were not boys, but in their late teens and even twenties. Monks recalled the gangfight only a couple of nights before, and wondered, not for the first time, how much of that war had been about old men wanting young men out of the way.

Alison was late. As the minutes passed, his tension moved into concern, then worry. But then he spotted her, a slender figure in a tan raincoat. He strode toward her, raising his hand. When he embraced her, she leaned into him, but her body did not yield. Monks let her go.

He said, "We found more pieces. They're spinning around in the air, but they won't click together."

"Pieces like?"

He told her, keeping pace with her as she walked: noting that she moved toward the lights and crowds of the city rather than the sometimes isolated pathways of the campus.

"Stover wondered if Jephson might have used Springkell, maybe even still does," he finished. "Brainwashed him and controls him. Is that feasible?"

"I think it might be possible to get somebody to kill that way," Alison said. "But to expect him not to slip up, to stay stable and never reveal anything, would be very risky."

They reached Telegraph, stepping into the street to skirt vendors' booths, with traffic edging alongside, sociopathic bicyclists careening through, fresh-faced upwardly mobile youths brushing shoulders with street people clad in outlandish combinations of garments, like primitives just touched by civilization.

Back on the sidewalk, Alison stopped and shook loose a cigarette.

"Worst city in the world to do this in. I won't make it to the end of the block before somebody starts in on me."

Monks took her lighter. She leaned in against the wind. That was when he saw the carefully applied makeup over the swollen right side of her jaw. He touched it with his finger, and noticed now that her coat was buttoned all the way to her chin, with the collar turned up. He pulled it away and saw the bruises spreading down her neck, and the torn blouse.

"It happened on the ward," she said. "That man I told you about, Garlick. I've been threatened before. Never touched."

Monks became aware that the anger which was always in him was building to rare intensity. "Did it have anything to do with this?"

"It will as soon as he talks to Jephson. I tried to get him to admit what's going on. I used the name Naia."

"Come with me, right now," Monks said. "My place is safe. We'll go to the FBI, get you out of sight until she's caught."

"What if she's not?"

Monks said, "I could go with you. We could find a place to stay, maybe out of the country. See how we get along."

"Oh, Rasp." Her tone was exasperated, even amused by the absurdity of the idea. "That's sweet," she added quickly, and kissed him, a peck on the cheek. "I've arranged to stay with a girl-friend the next few nights. Don't worry, I'll be around people all the time."

Monks pulled away and stood with his back half-turned, as if to conceal the bitter wound.

"You can't just keep on as if nothing's happened, Alison."

"She wants to get close to me. I'm going to find out who she is."

"Yeah? And then what?"

"I don't know. But she's not going to hurt me. We have the same thing in us. The mirror, except we're opposites. I've given into it, been passive. She's fighting."

"That's what you're supplying. What we *know* is that she has killed and possibly tortured several people."

"Suppose you'd been terribly injured. Someone you loved was murdered. Maybe you even witnessed it. Can you imagine what that would do to you?"

"Where the hell are you getting *that*?"

"If I run, or get the police after her," she said, "that's what's going to get me hurt."

She inhaled the last of the cigarette and dropped it in a street trash basket, its bottom sticky with residue, wire-mesh sides dented from vehicles or human feet expressing rage.

"The strangest thing in all of this?" she said.

"I'm starting to realize I might just have saved Garlick's life."

She stepped into the street ahead of a car. Monks had to wait for it and several more. On the other side she turned to face him, touching in him a memory of a myth, lovers separated by a treacherous sea channel that the young man swam every night until he drowned in a storm.

When Monks walked into his house, depression laid on him like a heavy blanket across his shoulders, the likes of which he had not experienced in years: the absurd vanity of a middle-aged man who had allowed himself to think that he might have been something to her besides useful.

He started a fire, fed the cats, poured a drink, and punched the PLAY button on his answering machine.

"Carroll, it's Roman Kasmarek. I got the PM for Robby Vandenard. From what I can glean, the evidence for suicide is persuasive, but circumstantial. Robby left a suicide note and wandered away from the family estate. He wasn't found for several months. There was bad decomposition and damage from animals and the wound itself, but he was carrying identification, and still holding his father's shotgun.

"Hope that helps. I'll be at the hospital till five."

Monks found a legal pad and clipboard and sat

on the couch, trying to recall information as it had come.

Alison Chapley stumbles onto the false diagnoses and unjustified releases of several NGIs. It seems clear that this has been calculatingly arranged by Dr. Francis Jephson.

She confronts Jephson obliquely. He claims ignorance, but soon afterward, a private investigator makes inquiries about Alison's personal life, presumably with the aim of damaging her professionally. She assumes that Jephson is behind this.

In an attempt to protect herself, she goes looking for information that might compromise Jephson in return. She learns that Robby Vandenard, heir to a wealthy San Francisco family, killed a man in 1984, and Jephson was instrumental in getting Robby the NGI verdict. Not long afterward, Jephson's prestigious JCOG program was founded—with Vandenard money—and Robby was one of the first admissions, thus being guaranteed release after an easy two years instead of a much longer term in a maximum security institution.

But Robby committed suicide not long after his release. Or did Jephson engineer his murder, fearing exposure?

Monks and Larrabee call on Darla Lutey, wife of the hired hand Robby Vandenard shot. She gives them reason to think that Robby was also falsely diagnosed by Jephson, was in fact a sociopath. But the real shock: suspicion that at age eleven, Robby had murdered his fourteen-year-old sister Katherine.

Alison is called in by Francis Jephson and offered a promotion, in what clearly seems to be a bribe for silence. She refuses. That afternoon, she finds a photograph of child killer Caymas Schulte in her car, with the suggestion that someone wants to give her information.

Monks and Larrabee learn from Dennis O'Dwyer that Jephson's connection with Robby Vandenard goes far back: Jephson treated Robby at the time of his sister's murder.

In Mendocino, Monks and Alison meet Caymas's frightened and abused younger brother, Tanager. He tells them about a woman named Naia, who said she was from "the hospital" Caymas had supposedly been taken to, and who paid for a motorcycle in return for showing her Caymas's hideout. It seemed that Naia had enlisted Caymas to damage or murder someone, but that he had blackmailed her instead. Caymas was now presumed dead.

Tanager leads them, too, to Caymas's hideout. They find the gift that Naia left for Alison: a death mask of Caymas Schulte, together with his baseball cap—and a mirror painted so as to ring Alison's eyes with blood.

Bernard Capaldi obliquely admits string-pulling to get Robby Vandenard the NGI verdict. He confirms and emphasizes the closeness between Robby and Jephson. He does not deny that Jephson may even have influenced Robby to murder.

Monks gets autopsy reports from Roman Kasmarek indicating that two of the four other NGIs may have been killed, too—disabled and brutalized first.

The spotlight, by now, is clearly on Francis Jephson. He is certainly culpable of unethical behavior. Robby Vandenard was in a position to compromise him, even have him sent to prison, thus giving Jephson an excellent motive to kill Robby—and perhaps to continue on, to eliminate a similar risk with other NGIs.

Monks and Larrabee check out a missing NGI file: Thomas Springkell, who was a friend of Robby Vandenard. Robby reneged on the friendship after his release; Tommy got depressed and disappeared. Larrabee brings up the possibility that Jephson has used Tommy to kill.

And now, Alison is convinced that she is safe. Naia will reveal herself to Alison soon. To start a law enforcement search or try to hide could be disastrous.

Monks got up and poured another drink, admitting in the confessional of his heart that if Naia was only killing men like those NGIs, it would not be hard to look the other way.

Inside her house, Alison poured a glass of chilled chardonnay and ran a bath. Her fingers traced the dark bruises on her face, neck and between her breasts where she had taken Garlick's knee. The thought came that they were stigmata, tangible signs of an unseen power marking her.

She had lied to a man who had treated her with nothing but kindness—hurt him deliberately. In part, she had done it to protect him.

But, mostly she had done it to keep him from interfering. The lifetime of dammed-up emotion that she had only acted out in tawdry, cowardly games, was finally breaking free. This afternoon, with the takedown of John James Garlick, she had sent her own message back to Naia: she was ready.

The quail was growing teeth.

She dried and walked to her bedroom, to where she had hidden the gifts under a pile of unused clothes in a trunk. She took the mask back to the living room, turned down the lights, and sat by the phone like a schoolgirl, gazing into the mirror with the blood-red rings around her own eyes, waiting for a reply.

Late that night the devil came to Monks in shadowy form and offered him a deal: no catch, straight across, quid pro quo.

For Monks, complete oblivion. Annihilation of being. Rest.

The price: that he would be powerless ever again to help anyone he cared about. His children, Alison, the sick and the wounded: anyone he might ever lay hands on would just have to get along without him from now on.

In his half-sleep, surrounded by cats that seemed strangely alert, he nodded, and reached out to sign the pact. It was the best offer he had ever gotten. Everything he had ever done or could foresee doing amounted to fuck-all anyway.

But caution had been driven into him too hard over the years. His hand pulled back.

Let me think about it.

It's a one-time offer, came the warning. *It's what you want most. You know it and I know it.*

I need to think.

When he awoke, it was gone.

13

Alison dreamed of water, of drifting along a clear murmuring stream that gathered in the near but unseen distance to a rushing cascade. As she began to wake, she was no longer on the water but in it, swimming her way to the surface, finally breaking into consciousness. For several heartbeats, the part of her mind that was usually in charge, the pilot, stayed missing: off behind a wall, doing something unknowable.

Then, with the instant shock of panic, it was back.

There was water running somewhere in the house.

For seconds longer she lay without moving, straining to hear other sounds over her own quiet, tight breathing. It was deep night, with only the dim light she had left on in the kitchen when she had given up and gone to bed.

She put on a robe and stepped carefully to her bedroom doorway. As she leaned into the hall the sound jumped louder in her ears: a cheerful steady splashing. It was not from either bathroom. She crossed the hall in slow silent steps and waited. No other noise came, no shadows moved.

The dining area was empty, undisturbed, her purse on the kitchen counter where she had left it. She stepped past and peered around the cabinets to the living room. Fresh sea breeze touched her face. Curtains were blowing gently.

The French doors onto the deck were open wide. The splashing was coming from the Jacuzzi outside.

She stood absolutely still. Two minutes. Three. A sudden buzz made her knees jerk, almost buckling them. It was the refrigerator kicking on.

The switch to the deck's single light was beside the open doors. She flicked it on, her gaze searching rapidly. There was no one in the Jacuzzi, no crouched figure clinging to the railing. The drop was almost twenty feet to the bluff below.

Then she looked back at what her gaze had at first refused to acknowledge. Perched on the tub's edge was a silver tray. It held an ice bucket containing a misted bottle of Veuve Clicquot champagne, two fluted glasses, and a white gift box, eight or ten inches square.

She turned once, staring into the blankness of the house behind her. Then she stepped out and opened the box.

Her fingers parted the tissue inside and looked down at a chalk-white plaster mask of a man's face. His features were agonized, his teeth clamped in a snarl.

Garlick.

She touched the mask to lift it. Her fingers indented the still soft plaster. Beneath it, they brushed something soft and bristly, like fur. They pulled back of themselves. The touch was not unpleasant: it was wrong. An odd sweetish smell, real or imagined, came to her nostrils. She held her breath, lifted the mask aside, and peered close.

There was just enough light to make out a patch of spiky dark hair, a frayed edge of skin, a bloody mass of paper towels beneath.

Very carefully, Alison replaced the mask over this mortal remnant of John James Garlick, gripper of women's hair, and backed into the house.

"Are you here?" she said. "Are you listening?"

She turned as she spoke, moving a careful step at a time.

"I can't accept this gift. Don't be angry."

She reached the kitchen counter. Nothing moved. With measured slowness, she picked up her purse, clasped it under her arm, and started toward the front door.

"Please let me go," she said. "You're right, I'm a quail. I know now. That's all I'll ever be."

She closed the door quietly behind her and walked, a little more quickly, down the endless path between the thick, shadowed oleanders to her Mercedes.

The car's inside light came on with the open door. Seats and floor were empty. She slid in, moving fast now. Shaking fingers jammed the key into the ignition. She sobbed with relief when the engine caught, threw the gearshift into reverse, wheeled around to face the black swells of Bolinas Bay, with San Francisco rising like a fairy kingdom of light as far away as the moon. The road to town was unlit and deserted. The rearview mirror showed only the pale oval of her own reflection.

A sharp curve made her slow down. In the same instant, she became aware of a rustling, leathery sound behind her. Her gaze lifted again to the mirror.

This time, the glittering eyes staring back were not her own.

She jammed on the brake and grabbed for the door handle, but a gloved hand gripped her jaw and the sharp sting of a needle pierced her neck. The hands went to the steering wheel, closing over her own.

The car coasted to the side of the road.

Monks became aware of a heavy weight on his chest, and paws kneading his skin insistently. His hand found the cat and identified it by touch: Omar, the big blue Persian. He tried to quell its stirring, but Omar was agitated and would not stop.

Then the phone rang. He opened his eyes. His bedroom and the world outside were dark. It was 5:17 A.M.

He groped for the phone and said, "Hello."

"There's someone here who'd like to talk to you." The voice that spoke was high, hollow, eerily childlike. There was a humming, rumbling in the background. Machinery. A moving car.

Monks said, "Who is this?"

"Don't you know?"

He sat up, aware of a rippling through the hairs on his forearms. Omar jumped clear of him but stayed on the bed, watching him with the solemn round eyes of an owl.

"Who's the someone?"

"Your little psychologist friend."

"Put her on."

"Just a moment," the voice said with a secretarial air.

Seconds passed. Then he began to hear snuffling sounds of increasing urgency: the phone held close to the face of someone choking. In the background, the high, reedy voice crooned something that sounded like an aria.

Monks shouted, *What are you doing?*

Abruptly the choking sounds burst open into gasps, the hacking cough of a woman frantically sucking for breath. The singing stopped.

"I'm afraid she's not at her best right now."

He stared into the darkness, trying to keep his own breathing calm.

He said, "She's done no harm, to you or anyone else. She trusts you, cares about you. She knows you've been badly hurt."

"I care about *her*. I'm making her dream come true."

"You can't believe that. You're forcing her."

"She's just confused. Quite understandable."

Monks swallowed tightly and waited.

"You're her lover?"

"We were close."

"She lied to me about you, the little bitch," the voice, but sounding amused now.

"It's over between us."

The car sounds diminished, as if the vehicle was slowing, pulling to the roadside.

"Why did it end? If I'm not being too personal."

"She was—exploring. In ways that became unsettling to me."

"Because of what you saw in her?"

"No," Monks said. "In myself."

"Very perceptive. Very honest," the voice said, thoughtful now.

"You know, I really don't meet that many interesting people these days."

He said, "I'm not opposed to your work."

The ignition sounds died off. There came the clicks of an opening car door.

"She's going to be missed, soon," Monks said. "You can't just make someone like her disappear."

"I don't intend to make her disappear. I intend to make her understand something."

Another metallic sound: creaking. A trunk opening.

"I can have every police unit in California looking for her in sixty seconds."

"Really. It pains me to be taken for an amateur."

"Nobody knew about you until now. Somewhere, you left tracks."

A weary exhalation. "Hold on just a minute, will you?"

A murmur in the background, away from the phone: "Here we go, dear."

Shuffling, rustling, the sounds of something heavy being moved. Monks gripped the phone, fearing he had lost contact. He strained to hear, willed the line to stay open. Ten seconds. Twenty.

The background murmur again:

"Whoops, almost forgot your present."

Then, the unmistakable *whump* of a closing trunk.

"Don't crowd me, Monks," the voice said, cold and edged now. "No official involvement. Believe me, I have ears in many places.

"Oh, yes. I left you something in her house, just by way of insurance."

"What do you mean, *insurance*?"

The line went dead.

Instantly, Monks punched Star–69. There came static, a pause, and then a woman's stern voice, sounding as if she was scolding a child:

"That number cannot be traced. Hang up now."

For seconds longer, his finger stayed poised to punch the numbers 911.

He slammed his open hand down on the nightstand, pulled on jeans and shirt, and ran for the Bronco. Omar darted in and out between his feet, something Monks had never known him to do. He swore and swept the cat aside with his ankle, then looked up and stopped hard.

There was just enough moonlight through the clouds to illuminate the two other cats, on top of the vehicle's hood, facing the windshield. Like worshippers in some witchy rite, they crouched belly low, then leaped high into the air, hunched, ears flat and tails stiff. Low, menacing wails erupted into sudden screams and spitting.

Monks stepped forward carefully.

Something was moving in the front seat: a slim, upright shadow that weaved from side to side with alarming swiftness.

His mouth opened. He stepped closer.

The shadow lunged forward in a dark blur, sending both cats howling and leaping. There was a thump against the windshield, then a slimy stain dripping down.

The regal hooded shape of a cobra's head remained poised, weaving furiously.

Monks walked away, dropped to his knees, and vomited. He remained there for perhaps three minutes, head in hands, body jerking in random shivers. Then he returned, crouching, to the cats.

"Come on, you guys," he said quietly. "This is mine now. Come on, you've done your job." He encircled them with his outstretched arms, drawing them in, flinching as the cobra attacked the windshield when his hands got close. The cats struggled, but allowed themselves to be gripped.

Inside the house, he blocked the cat door and spooned out large portions of fresh food. He brushed his teeth and rinsed his face, and went to the safe for his shotgun.

Monks gathered a powerful flashlight and several white bedsheets, and walked back outside, remembering things he had read about cobras. They were fearless and aggressive; the word "insolent" was frequently used. One description from an Englishman in India spoke of a released snake entering a house "like an arrow from a bow." Some species could spit blinding venom at a victim's eyes, ten or fifteen feet with pinpoint accuracy. Bites not treated immediately usually brought death, in agony, within hours. Monks had seen a couple in captivity in Asia himself, and the overwhelming impression was that they were made to kill, and they knew it.

He circled the Bronco again, with the flashlight close to the windows. The cobra followed,

upright head lunging to stay with the light.
There seemed to be only the one; no other
shapes came into view.

He spread the bedsheets on the ground outside the driver's door, giving him a twenty-foot
radius of light-colored surface. He positioned the
flashlight on the ground to illuminate it. He
jacked a round into the shotgun's chamber and
clicked off the safety. He hyperventilated three
times.

Then he stepped in, yanked open the door,
and leaped back.

The snake came out like a dark streak, moving
in a rippling line of impossible swiftness. It had
almost reached the cover of night when Monks
fired. It reared up, head twisting, then flopped
down, writhing.

He stepped closer and aimed carefully. The
second shot flopped it over again. This time it lay
still except for the eerie squirming of muscles
triggered by nerves that did not yet know their
brain was dead.

He walked around the Bronco again, thump-
ing and kicking, then opened the other door and
tailgate and searched with the flashlight. There
was nothing visible.

Monks gathered up the still jerking snake in
the bedsheets, careful to avoid the fangs, and put
it in a closed garbage can. It was at least five feet
long, with a dense rubbery weight. He got surgi-

cal goggles and gloves and a bottle of ammonia, and swabbed the streaked venom off windows and dash.

Was that what Jephson had been doing with a rattlesnake when he was bitten?

Was he the phony detective who called himself Stryker?

Trying to catch it?

Practicing snake-handling?

Monks drove as fast as he could to Bolinas, shoulders tensed against the sight or sound of another weaving head that might have been lying hidden.

Monks arrived at Alison's house at 6:27 A.M. He sat in the Bronco for half a minute, grasping for the fantasy that this was all a dream or malarial hallucination, that this was all, he would ring the doorbell and she would answer, sweet with sleep, surprised but not displeased.

Gone to stay with a friend, she'd said.

And he had believed her.

It was still night, the house dimly lit. With flashlight and shotgun, he scanned the ground for twisting shapes in the grass. *Insurance*.

There was no alarm system. Years ago, he had lobbied to get her to put one in, but she was convinced that she could not be touched.

He tried the front doorknob cautiously. It was unlocked.

An invitation to him, from Naia.

He shoved the door open, gun ready. The kitchen area was still, with a single light on over the counter. Nothing seemed out of place.

He walked down the hall, checking the empty rooms. Her bedroom was the last. On a chair, he recognized the clothes she had worn yesterday, with the torn blouse trailing to the floor. The bed was neatly made, and Monks almost missed the tiny face that smiled up from a pillow.

He stepped forward, staring. It was an antique china doll, with hand-painted porcelain face and real blond hair, tucked into the bed like a child.

Recognition hit his heart like a hammer. A doll that had belonged to his ex-wife's great-grandmother, passed down through the generations of women to his daughter Stephanie.

Monks turned, sweeping the room slowly with his shotgun, finger on the trigger, about to shoot at something, anything in futile rage.

He put the weapon down and, with shaking hands, phoned his ex-wife's home in Davis. His eyes went damp with relief when Stephanie answered. In the background, he could hear the sounds of breakfast.

"Daddy, what are you doing calling so early?"

"Stef, this is very important. Where do you keep Grandma Annie's china doll?"

Pause. "In my bedroom. In the closet. Why?"

"I'm afraid somebody took it."

"*What?*"

Monks listened helplessly to her sharp breathing as she hurried down the hall to check. A door banging. The sounds of rustling cloth. And then, Stephanie's panicked voice:

"She's *gone*."

"Here's what I need you to do, baby. You and your mom get some clothes together, enough for a few days, and get to another city. Vegas, L.A., someplace not around here. Find a nice hotel, go shopping, whatever you want. I'm going to pick up the bill."

"Daddy, I can't just leave in the middle of the semester—"

"Stef, I'll work this out with your teachers. You've got to do this and you've got to do it *right now*. Remember Dr. Kasmarek? When you get there, call him and tell him where you are. *Don't* call my phone for any reason. Okay?"

"What *is* this?"

"I'm dealing with somebody dangerous. I can't believe it's spilled over onto you, but it's a fact. We've got to get you safe, and then we'll worry about the rest."

"Why *me*?"

"I know some things about this person. He's trying to keep me from going to the police."

"Daddy, how long is this going to last?" Her voice was breaking with panic now. "If they don't catch him, does that mean—"

Monks squeezed his temples with his fingers,

weighing the value of lying to lessen her fear, but gave it up.

"You'd better put your mom on."

In the background, he could hear Stephanie trying to explain to her mother, and Gail's questions rising in quantum leaps from incredulity to fury, along with the harrumphing of her new husband, Barry.

Gail's voice cut into the phone. "Carroll, what in the *hell* have you gotten us into now?"

"There's no time to argue, Gail. I'll explain as soon as I can, but right now you've got to get out of there. Take Barry too, if you want."

"Is this for real? You've got someone stalking us? Who's been in my *house*?"

Monks started to say, *For Christ's sake, I didn't ask for it*, but remained silent.

"This is our *life*, dammit," she said. He could hear her anger giving way to tears. "That's all I ever wanted: a normal life. What do I have to *do*?"

The line went dead.

Monks walked to the French doors and pulled back a curtain. The sky was turning faintly lighter with the dawn.

For the first time in his life, he wanted to kill.

He picked up the phone and called Stover Larrabee.

The weight of consciousness was returning to Alison, a reluctant awakening from a long dream that could not be recalled. At some point she realized that her eyes were open, but trying to move was too much effort. Her mind absorbed what she saw, without supplying emotions or logic. She was lying in a semidark room. There were several stuffed animals on the bed with her. The walls were papered in a pastel blue pattern, with a shelf of dolls and another of old LP records.

"Are we awake?" a familiar high-pitched voice said. It was soft now, soothing. A hand stroked her hair. "We'll have to let this grow out, like it used to be."

Then the hand tightened, yanking a fistful of hair, making her inhale sharply with pain.

"*What* got into you? This was all going so beautifully."

The grip tightened further, making her gasp again, then let go. The bed shifted, releasing the weight of the person who had been sitting by her head.

"Let's get you dressed properly," the voice said. "There's someone coming to see you. Someone who's going to make you feel very different."

The hands pulled her bathrobe away, off her arms, out from under her. Then a nightgown came to replace it, pulled down over her head and neck. It was fine white linen trimmed with pink, with a little girl's bow at the bosom.

When it reached her hips, there was a pause. One of the hands touched her hesitantly between the thighs, a timid gesture that was not even a caress. It rested there, unmoving, for several seconds. She was aware of slow, controlled breathing. Then the hand withdrew, and pulled the gown on down to her ankles.

"Now," the voice whispered. "Tell me all about the games you like to play."

14

Monks waited for Larrabee in a shopping center parking lot in Orinda, sipping bad convenience store coffee. The gray morning had dawned, and the sky was heavy with rolling clouds that threatened more rain. On the seat beside him rested a Clevinger Hospital directory that he had taken from Alison's desk, with Francis Jephson's unlisted address. He had circled the location on a map. It was about a mile away.

A few minutes after eight A.M., an older van, dented and long unwashed, pulled in. It carried lengths of copper and PVC pipe on the rack, and bore the logo: "ON THE SPOT" PLUMBING. Larrabee walked to the Bronco, wearing a brown duck jacket, baseball cap, and coveralls. Like Monks, he needed a shave.

Larrabee leaned against the Bronco and folded his arms.

"A fucking *cobra*?"

"It would have gotten me for sure, except for the cats."

"Carroll. This has changed. You're out of your league, way out."

"I know that, Stover. But I'm afraid to make the wrong phone call. And I have no idea which call that is. If Naia gets wind the police are after her, my family might have to stay in hiding."

Larrabee was watching him, a look Monks had seen before, grim and disconcerting, and he knew Larrabee was thinking the same thing: How long could you hide from someone like Naia?

"That's not exactly what I'm getting at," Larrabee said. "She's gone to a lot of trouble to let you know that isn't about harming Dr. Chapley, right?"

"She half-asphyxiated Alison, making sure I heard."

"I don't doubt she's capable of it. But it's not what she wants."

"Meaning?"

"Stealing your daughter's doll, having that all set up," Larrabee said. "You realize it means Naia's known who you were at least since yesterday, maybe longer. *Before* she grabbed Dr. Chapley. How do you figure that?"

Monks had been thinking about it.

"There are several possibilities. That kid in Mendocino could still have been in touch with Naia. Given her my license number."

"Maybe. Or maybe you're risking yourself and your family for somebody who hasn't been straight with you. Maybe Dr. Chapley and Naia have something going on their own. If you want to let them work it out, I never heard of it."

Monks had been thinking about that too.

He said, "Maybe they do. Let's see what we turn up with Jephson."

He handed Larrabee a photograph of Alison that he had found in her house. It apparently had been taken on a hiking trip or picnic. She was smiling, fresh, with windblown hair.

Larrabee examined it. "Not bad."

"I looked for the things Naia had given her. That death mask and cap. They're hidden or gone. The phone machine tape was blank."

Larrabee checked his watch. "Let's start by finding out if Jephson's at work."

Monks locked the Bronco and got into the plumbing van. Larrabee set the radio-phone on speaker and punched the number. A middle-aged woman answered: "Dr. Jephson's office."

"Good morning. This is Kenneth Hahn, from Mother Lode Realty in Concord. May I speak to—" Larrabee paused, as if reading the name "—Dr. Francis Jepson, please?"

"Dr. *Jephson* is not available." Her voice was cool, defensive, pointedly correcting the pronunciation. "Is there something I can help you with?"

"I'm calling to make an inquiry, ma'am. A client—I suppose I should say, a potential client, a very wealthy one—has approached us with an aggressive interest in purchasing Dr. Jephson's house. Now, we realize it's not formally for sale, but the terms would be extremely advantageous to him. Can you tell me when you expect him back?"

She hesitated. "He called in last night to say he had a family emergency. He's likely to be gone for several days."

Larrabee's lips pulled back from his teeth in a humorless grin.

"I'm sorry to hear that. I'll try him next week."

He switched off the phone and said, "All right, let's cruise the house. You stay out of sight."

Monks crouched in the back of the van, peering out the rear windows. Jephson's house was on a sedate street, with spacious yards and hedges. Larrabee drove past at moderate speed. A newspaper lay on the doorstep. There were no visible lights on inside. It did not look like anyone had spent the night there.

"It doesn't feel right," Larrabee said. "Naia's got to have a place where she can do whatever she's doing to those guys, break bones, make them crawl. Messy and noisy. This looks like it's built on a slab. Not even a basement."

An image rose in Monks's mind of Alison, locked in some dank warehouse or deserted farm building. Waiting.

"You want to go in?" Larrabee said. "If we get busted, I might or might not be able to talk us out of it. Either way, the cops are in it from there."

Monks said, "I can't not."

Larrabee swung the van in a U-turn, then pulled into Jephson's driveway.

"I'm going back to see if there's an alarm system. If anybody comes by, Jephson called us to ream out the sewer line. You hang here and rummage with the tools. Let people see you."

He pointed at another pair of overalls, hanging from a hook. Monks put them on and spent the next minutes leaning into the van's sliding doors, pretending to arrange tools, keeping a tense watch for an approaching squad car. The neighborhood stayed quiet.

Larrabee returned. "The bad news is, it's a microprocessor. I can't just nick a wire. The good is, it's an old Radionics system. I might be able to get into the panel."

He opened a greasy toolbox and handed Monks a locator wand, then opened another box himself. In it was a laptop computer with attached phone.

Monks prowled the yard, wand in hand, as if searching for the buried sewer pipe, while Larrabee punched numbers and listened. Three cars passed during the minutes, but none slowed.

Larrabee closed the box. "I think I got it. We're going to stay right here in front. If I fucked up, we've got maybe sixty seconds before it goes off, and then it'll probably only sound at the security company. We leave like nothing's happened."

He walked to the door holding what looked like a small pistol. He fit the barrel onto the deadbolt and paused.

"You know what I was going to do today? Meet a guy who's got a '66 BSA Victor to sell. I had one when I was eighteen."

There came a quiet *thud* that Monks felt more than heard.

Larrabee moved the barrel to cover the main lock. The *thud* came again. The door swung silently open. He stepped to a wall-mounted panel with a keypad and nodded.

"We're clear. Welcome to the wonderful world of tampering with evidence." He took a packet of surgical gloves from his pocket and handed a pair to Monks.

They walked quickly through the house. It was furnished with carefully selected antiques: tasteful, fussy. The bed was made, with no sign of hasty exit or disturbance. Larrabee was right: there was no basement. They pulled open closets as they walked. There were no obvious signs of women's clothing.

The answering machine light was blinking in Jephson's home office. Larrabee punched the PLAY button.

"Dr. Jephson, this is Mrs. Brill, at Clevinger Hospital. The night nursing supervisor? We know you're out of town, Doctor, but we've been unable to reach you at the number you left. We hope you'll pick up this message. I'm calling to issue you a Tarasoff warning."

Monks knew the term: a state-mandated warning to mental institution personnel, when an inmate who had threatened them was at large.

"John James Garlick escaped sometime last night. He's considered very dangerous, especially because he was involved in a violent incident earlier that afternoon. Police are alerted and the area is being searched, but we urge you to take precautions for your personal safety.

"Please call us at your earliest opportunity. The police are anxious to talk to you."

The machine clicked. A digital voice said: "Friday, 7:14 A.M. You have no more messages."

Monks said, "The violent incident was with Alison. Garlick attacked her."

"And it sounds like Jephson left a bogus phone number."

Larrabee yanked open a file drawer. It was packed with manila folders.

"It'd take for fucking ever to get through all this," he said. "Let's do the desk. Look for an address book, personal letters, anything like that."

Monks scanned a desktop basket of correspondence. It was all professional. The drawers held office supplies and stationery, all impersonal items.

"He's not keeping anything important here," Larrabee said. "The whole thing, even the alarm system, is set up to make him look like a model citizen."

On their way out, Larrabee stepped to the television and slipped a finger into the VCR's door. He stopped and ejected a cassette. It was unlabeled.

"Let's just see what kind of home movies the doc's been watching." He rewound the tape several seconds. Monks stepped to a window and twitched the curtain aside. The street was still quiet.

The TV screen lit. Larrabee started the tape.

They stared at the image that appeared:

A powerfully built man, his back to the camera, hanging upside down by one roped foot like a swordfish or a deer. The other thigh jutted out horizontally, but from the knee down the leg dangled so as to suggest that it had been partially severed. The torso bore several long slashes. Both pants and shirt were soaked with blood. On the room's stone floor lay a crumpled baseball cap. The body was twisting very slowly, and Monks did not think he was imagining that it was still jerking in final, futile attempts to escape.

Larrabee shoved the tape in his pocket. They strode for the door.

Back in the parking lot, Larrabee slumped in the driver's seat, fingers drumming on the dash. "*This* will put Jephson in jail."

Monks was trying to erase mental images: the slowly twisting body with its flopping hamstrung leg, hung upside down, like the searcher Caymas Schulte had caught in a snare and almost beaten to death.

The blood-soaked crotch of a child rapist.

Monks said, "We've still got to find him."

"He's more scared than he wants you to think. Leaving that tape was a big mistake."

Monks had brought the retrieval code from Alison's answering machine. He said, "Let's see if she got one of those Tarasoff warnings."

She had, along with one more message. The voice was a man's: not young, probably black, definitely uneasy.

"Alison, it's Harold. The hospital says you haven't checked in. I need to know you're all right. Please call me, I'm at home." The phone number he left belonged to one Harold Henley, 3718 Cambridge, Richmond.

Larrabee said, "I'll get this tape home and see what else is on it."

Monks trotted to the Bronco.

Cambridge turned out to be a side street in Richmond, several blocks west of San Pablo. The neighborhood was residential, mostly fifties-vintage homes of aging pastel stucco, with an occasional two- or three-story apartment building. There was a small grocery-liquor store on one corner, with wire-grilled windows and two men out front who seemed pointedly unaware of Monks's passage.

He found the address two blocks farther down: one of the apartment buildings, well-kept and recently painted. Through the driveway into the courtyard parking lot, he caught a glimpse of stacked lumber, rolls of insulation, other building materials. A door on the ground floor just off the main entry had a MANAGER sign and a glass peephole. It was 8:52 A.M. Monks rang the bell.

He could feel the vibration of heavy footsteps approaching the door. Fifteen seconds passed, while he felt himself scrutinized. Then came the sounds of locks turning, a chain being undone, and Monks found himself looking at a man so large he almost stepped back.

"Mr. Henley?"

Harold Henley's chin lifted slightly. He was wearing a light blue nylon jogging suit with white stripes and bedroom slippers. His eyes were watchful.

"I'm here about Alison."

A tremor passed across Harold's face, but control returned instantly. "Alison who?"

"Alison who you just called half an hour ago."

Harold moved as if to close the door.

Monks said forcefully, "Somebody's got her. A killer."

The tremor came again. Harold's mouth opened. He made a sudden panting sound.

"I'm not police, I'm her friend," Monks said. "You *have* to tell me what you know."

"Oh, man." The words came out like a sob. The huge body turned away, leaving the door open. Monks stepped in after him and closed it behind.

The air in the apartment was pervaded by the sweetish scent of fresheners, and the furnishings suggested an almost comic fantasy of a swinging bachelor life: eggshell-white shag carpet, black leather couch, portable bar displaying expensive liquors, and a Sony entertainment center with a screen three feet across. But the sense was broken by the room's central feature, an overstuffed chair pulled up close to the TV, and scalloped deeply by a great lonely weight.

Harold said, "You haven't told me your name."

"Monks."

"You her man?"

Monks hesitated. "No."

Harold moved to a window and stood with his back to the room. Narrowly parted Levelor blinds showed the courtyard, where the comings and goings of tenants would be most visible. It was another place he seemed to spend a lot of time.

"World treats black people different than white people. Where you live, Monks? You got crackheads hanging on your street corners? You scared to open a window?"

Monks's gaze flicked to the door, which bore several deadbolts and hasps.

"I sold TVs, cars," Harold said. "Finally bought this place. It was trash. I been fixing it up. Another couple years, I'll be able to buy me a house someplace I don't have to worry about that shit."

Monks waited. The air fresheners cloyed. His armpits were unpleasantly damp.

"Most white people treat black people different, too. You understand, Monks?"

"I don't like it either, Harold. But Alison's not that way. Is she?"

"Suppose I tell you something. How much you going to help me?"

"If we get her back safe, I never heard of you."

"Ain't going to help me with *some*body that's heard of me."

Monks said, "Who?"

"Name that start with a N."

Comprehension began in Monks's mind.

"Tell me," he said. "Say the name."

Harold neither moved nor spoke. It was sinking in that he possessed a deliberateness that was as much a part of him as his huge bones.

A deliberateness compounded by fear.

Monks said, "Naia. That's who's got her, Harold. Did you know that too?"

Finally Harold half turned. His face was deeply creased.

"Patient escaped last night. Man named Garlick."

"The one who attacked Alison?"

Nod. "Hospital found him missing early this morning. I took the day off to look after my personal safety. Called her to see if she's all right. That's what I could tell the police, Monks."

Monks waited again, while Harold planned his words or simply decided enough time had passed to continue.

"Way it started out, I gave information. That's all. Came out to my car after work one day. Be eight years now. Car was locked, but there was a envelope on the floor. Five thousand dollars cash and a note, that all it said was the location of a phone booth and a time.

"Phone rang right on the minute. A woman's voice, except you could tell it wasn't real. She told me the kind of thing she want to know. Who the NGIs were. What they'd done. When and where they were released. Another five thousand every time. You would of done it too, Monks."

So: Harold Henley had not bought and remodeled an apartment building just on a security guard's salary. He had been selling information to Naia.

Monks said, "Probably so."

"Then Alison had to come sniffing round."

Harold's head drooped, and Monks's scalp bristled with realization.

Harold had sold that information, too.

Monks said, "You son of a bitch."

He lunged forward and threw a punch, a wild

roundhouse right. It glanced off Harold's raised shoulder with the feel of hitting a slab of beef. Monks pulled in his elbows, fists beside his chin, ready for a desperate effort to keep the terrific body from bludgeoning him to the floor and crushing the life from him.

But Harold only made that strange panting sound again, and turned away.

"I *had* to, man. I couldn't lie to Naia. She'd kill me, too." Harold's hands opened as if to grip the empty air. "With those other men—it was not wrong. I never thought it would come round to Alison."

Monks moved away, trying to even his breathing. In the small room there was no place to go.

"Pretty soon Naia's crazy about Alison, man," Harold said. "Wants to know everything that happen with her."

And you kept adding up that five thousand dollars a pop, Monks thought.

"I told her about the fight with Garlick yesterday. She told me go back and get him."

Monks said, "Get him?"

"I said no way. You know what she did? She silent, man. She just stay there on the phone, not saying nothing. I wait ten seconds, twenty seconds, thinking about those men. Finally I say I'll try, and she just hang up.

"You understand, man? I didn't want to do this, but I got to. I went back late last night, pushing a laundry cart. Wedged open the fire door and waited till the nurse take her break. Told Garlick, 'I'm going to get you out of here, man,' so he'd come willingly. Put him in the trunk of my car."

"What did you do with him?"

"Parked my car where she told me. Dark parking lot. Gave him another shot of droperidol and left him. Come back a hour later and he's gone."

"And there was money instead?"

Harold's head did not move, either in assent or denial.

"I'm trying to add up the felonies, Harold."

"What I told you."

"You *knew* what Naia was doing to those men."

"Didn't *know*, but when you close to the ground, you hear things. Grapevine, you understand? Somebody catch a rumor in Sacramento that Prokuta drowned hisself, man who'd cut a baby's throat to stay alive. Kurlin gets caught in a fire, just like he used to do. Nobody puts it all together. Except Harold."

"Did you ever see Naia?"

The great head shook no.

"Could she be Jephson?"

"Got reasons why it could or couldn't be anybody."

"How did you get in touch with her? A phone number?"

"We just talking right now, Monks. Nobody can prove nothing about this. If I give you something, that's different. That's jail."

"This is about Alison, Harold. Alison, who

treated you right." He leaned into the averted face. "Alison, who you sold out."

Harold walked behind the bar. He held up an old-fashioned glass, offering it. Monks shook his head. Harold filled the glass to the brim with Chivas Regal and drank half of it.

"One day I come to my car and there's a extra five thousand. When I talk to her, she tells me she wants me to do something else this time. Man about to be released, Prokuta. Take him aside and tell him when he needs money, call Harold.

"He came around, couple months later. I gave him two hundred dollars and set up a place for Naia to meet with him. Never saw him no more. Did the same thing with two others.

"That's all I know till Hogface Foote calls me one night."

Monks searched his mind for the name and found it: the San Jose biker who had stabbed a college boy for sitting on his Harley.

"Motherfucker was scary, man," Harold said. "I give him four hundred. Few nights later he call me and *he's* scared. He says, 'Bitch knew it wasn't real. She wants a photo, man.'"

"I'm not following you, Harold."

"She was buying something from them, man. You understand? Something's been on somebody a while."

Monks said, "*On* somebody?"

"Trophy, you know? Ring. Hair. Something that's like part of them."

Monks stared in disbelief.

"I didn't want to know that and I wouldn't of, except Foote came by here that same night. High on crank, white all round his eyeballs. I wouldn't let him in. He shows me a picture through the door. Man lying in a alley in his own blood. Got a earring on, except now Foote got the earring in his hand, with a piece of ear still on it. Says, 'This is real, motherfucker.' I give him another hundred to get him gone, and tell him take it to her. Never see him no more neither."

Monks said, *"Why?"*

"Think about it, Monks. They all predators, man, they taking *life*. Most go after the weak, but she's going after the strong. Them. They stronger still if they just taken another life. Fatter."

Collecting human beings as trophies.

Creating a food chain of death that thrived on killers who had recently killed. Grown fat.

Harold filled his glass again. He replaced the bottle, opened a drawer, and laid a slip of paper on the bar. Then he walked to his chair and sat heavily.

Monks picked up the paper. On it was a nine-digit number, beginning with the 01 code of a foreign country.

Without turning, Harold said, "You going to use that number, Monks? Cause if you do—we not talking prison for Harold."

Monks glanced back as he closed the door.

The huge body remained seated, unmoving, facing the blank television screen.

Monks slid into the Bronco and gripped the cell phone that Larrabee had given him. He punched the numbers, making sure each one beeped, imagining electronic impulses like tiny streaks of light flashing thousands of miles through a network of connections, scramblers, blinds.

There came a series of clicks, a pause, and then a tone, short and harsh like a foghorn.

Monks said, in a voice that trembled with rage, "I found a track. If you come near my family again, I'll spend the rest of my life hunting you down."

15

The cell phone rang immediately, still in Monks's hand.

"Was it a big track? A black one?"

It was the same voice, high-pitched and arch, but with a subtly different quality this time: a faint distortion or echo. Perhaps a nontransmitting environment: basement, concrete room, freezer.

A place where a man could be hamstrung and forced to crawl.

Monks said, "Let me talk to her."

"I'm afraid she's not accepting calls just now."

"It's only a matter of time until this number's traced."

"If I thought that, I'd never have given it out."

"If you weren't worried, you wouldn't have called back."

"You're an unwelcome distraction to me, Dr. Monks, I admit it. I didn't expect to be hearing from you again. Nothing personal. What *did* happen to the snake?"

"It's dead."

"You know, I'm rather starting to like you. And here we both just want what's best for her. Shall we try to work this out, between us?"

"I'm listening."

"You want her back. But what makes you think she'd give me up? I'm what she's wanted all her life. What do *you* have to offer that can compare, in your grubby little world?"

Monks gazed around him at the bland houses and dreary streets, and it finally came to him that he had been wrong all the time. Alison Chapley's life was not the rich fest of pleasure and achievement that he had imagined, but an empty existence in a world that was going nowhere for someone who craved mystery, thrills—or perhaps, at the heart of it, escape.

She was not so different from him after all.

He said, "I could get a hundred thousand dollars within a few hours."

"Ransom?" the voice said thoughtfully.

"If you want to call it that."

"Interesting approach. I'm a firm believer that people should earn what they get. Don't you think?"

"In general. Yes."

"But let's not talk about money. That's too

easy. Let's talk risk. I've risked rather a great deal, to bring her to me. I think that gives me a certain right. How much are you willing to risk?"

Monks hesitated. "I don't know."

"Another honest answer. Let's say I propose a duel. A way to keep this between you and me."

"What weapons?"

"Brains. Nerve."

"Go on."

"I'll give you a challenge. A task. If you perform it, then you and I are quits. I'll give up my efforts to persuade our little friend."

Monks said, "What's the task?"

"I hold the prize," the voice said, edged. "I'll make the terms."

"That's one-sided. You have to ante up something, too. A reason to trust you."

"The task will provide another track. You'll have the chance to take it and walk away. Then *I* win. But if you cheat—take the information and stay in this—*I'll* be the one following tracks."

Monks finally said, "I accept."

"Be in San Francisco in exactly two hours. I'll call you at this number."

The connection ended.

He started for Larrabee's apartment.

The video was less than two minutes long. The first part showed Caymas Schulte, tethered by the neck to what looked like a warehouse rack.

Caymas's finger touched and sank into the white plaster mound at his place. A row of oval masks, bearing the grimacing features of the dead NGIs, stretched into the room's darkness.

Then a chalk-faced, dark-haired figure with blood-ringed eyes leaped onto the screen. A slashing movement of its arm severed the tether. Caymas backed away, with the figure following, holding a curved knife.

The film cut abruptly, showing only blank frames for another several seconds. Then came the image they had first seen: Caymas, hanging upside down, his blood pooling on the stone floor.

"She already tried to kill you once." Larrabee said. "You can't believe in that trust bullshit."

It was 10:32 A.M. The phone call was due at 11:07.

"I'm going to keep the connection open as long as I can. She might slip," Monks said.

Monks waited in the Bronco, parked along the Panhandle of Golden Gate Park. Larrabee was a block behind, driving the inconspicuous Taurus again.

Precisely at 11:07 A.M., the cell phone rang. The sound sent a rippling convulsion through his body. He clicked the phone on with his left hand, his right poised with pen and pad.

"This is Monks."

The high-pitched voice said, "You'll find what you're looking for in the parking lot of Mercy

Hospital. Instructions are included. When you're finished, call."

"How will I know what it is?"

"Oh, you'll know. Convincing photographs will serve as proof. I'd advise haste, Dr. Monks. The clock is running."

He accelerated into traffic, fighting the urge to floor it. He took his Beretta from the glove compartment and slipped it inside his belt under his sweatshirt. His gaze caught the antique straight razor that Alison had bought for him, the gift mocked by Naia's grim offerings. It fit neatly beside his wallet in the back pocket of his jeans.

Monks wheeled into the Mercy parking lot and drove through the sections, scanning the rows of vehicles.

Naia had been right: when he saw what he was looking for, he knew.

Alison's Mercedes, parked at the far west end.

He got out and trotted the last fifty feet, stomach queasy with fear at what he might find. Another deadly snake. A bomb or shotgun in his face.

Alison herself.

The car was empty. He stepped around to the trunk, inhaled deeply, and jerked it open.

The first thing he saw was scorch marks on the inside walls. The metal struts holding the backseat in place had been cut through with a torch. He gave the seat a push. It fell inward, opening a passage into the car.

Someone had gone to a lot of trouble to create a hiding place that would allow access to the interior.

His gaze moved to the trunk's well, neatly covered with a blanket. He pulled it off and stared down at a smallish figure, lying with back turned, knees drawn up toward the chest. He gripped the chin and pulled the face visible.

It was a white male, in his fifties, with fine features and light hair, wearing an expensive suit of dark wool.

Dr. Francis Jephson.

There was no sign of blood or a wound but he reeked of gin. Monks touched two fingers to the throat and felt a slow, strong pulse, leaned close and pried an eyelid open to reveal the small, sluggish pupil.

Alcohol and something else: a narcotic or benzodiazepine, like Valium.

A slip of paper that at first looked like a handkerchief was tucked into Jephson's breast pocket. Monks pulled it free.

CERTIFICATE OF DEATH
STATE OF CALIFORNIA
USE BLACK INK ONLY/NO ERASURES,
WHITEOUTS OR ALTERATIONS

NAME OF DECEDENT—FIRST (GIVEN)
FRANCIS

MIDDLE
SEWELL
LAST (FAMILY)
JEPHSON
DATE OF DEATH MM/DD/CCYY
11/14/1997
HOUR
12:11 PM
PLACE OF DEATH
MERCY HOSPITAL
IF HOSPITAL, SPECIFY ONE
ER/OP
ATTENDING PHYSICIAN'S NAME
CARROLL MONKS, M.D.

The space labeled DEATH WAS CAUSED BY was left blank.

But Monks's fingers had felt something else in the pocket, about the size of a film can, smooth and hard. He tugged it free. It was a multi-dose glass vial of potassium chloride.

His hands gripped the car frame. Thirty milligrams in solution, injected IV, would freeze the heart instantaneously, with the only trace a slight electrolyte imbalance in the blood. Death attributed to a coronary or stroke, a secondary complication of the presenting overdose.

Easy. And much easier still for Naia to have killed Jephson herself.

There was a reason she had set Monks up to do it, and the reason that reverberated in his brain came in the words of Harold Henley: *They stronger yet if they just taken another life. Fatter.*

Monks heaved Jephson up into a fireman's carry and headed for the Emergency Room in a lurching run.

The emergency staff at Mercy Hospital were not easily impressed, but the sight of one of their own doctors staggering in with a man over his shoulder caused a flutter. Aides came fast with a gurney. Monks leaned against a wall, fighting for breath

The on-duty physician, Jim Parrish, strode over to Monks.

"I found him outside," Monks said. "Somebody must have dumped him."

They moved along with the gurney, Parrish automatically checking vital signs. "What the hell are you doing here, Carroll?"

"I'm scheduled at noon. Aren't I?"

"I didn't think so." Parrish was in his thirties, competent and unimaginative. Although he had never said so, it was clear he was aware that Monks's reputation was not pristine.

Not the man Monks wanted in on this.

But he had seen, with a jolt of hope, that Vernon Dickhaut was here.

"Christ, I must have got my calendar wrong," Monks said. He had already read the ER: there were no visible crises, but it was crowded, and this being Friday, it would get more so.

They paused, both aware that Jephson's condition was serious but not critical. The aides wheeled the gurney on into a cubicle, a nurse following to start a workup.

Parrish said, "Alcohol and drugs?"

"Plenty of both, is my guess."

"He doesn't seem the type."

"Maybe a suicide attempt. You look busy, Jim. This might be a good one for Vernon. I could keep an eye on things. I mean, I found the guy." He hardened his gaze a notch. It was Parrish's ER, but he was senior.

Parrish shrugged, and waved his clipboard in a gesture of assent.

Monks caught Vernon's gaze and nodded him toward the cubicle. They met just outside the door. Monks blocked it casually, trying to look like an older doc giving a word of advice.

Very quietly, he said, "This isn't what it seems. I can't explain now, but in a few minutes I'm going to ask you to look the other way. Will you help?"

Vernon's sky-blue eyes widened to the point of goggling. For ten seconds, the two men looked into each other. Then Vernon nodded.

Monks said, "First guess is morphine or Demerol. Let's start with one milligram of Narcan, a five-second push, IV. Start lab, blood sugar, and do a urine-tox screen. He's drunk, too, so watch his breathing. If that doesn't start him around within two minutes, it might be Valium: try point-two milligrams of Romazicon. I'll be back in five."

Monks walked to the physicians' room, deliberately not moving too fast. Inside, he put on his lab coat, transferring the pistol to its pocket. It was 11:47 A.M.

He called Larrabee and said, "That was Jephson in the trunk."

"I saw you carry him in. Is he dead?"

"Not yet. That's the task."

There was a short but pointed silence, while Larrabee did not ask the question: *Is he going to be?*

Larrabee said, "She's got something in mind. Following you, waiting to pick you off."

"Let's let her follow. With you watching."

"I don't know how close I can stay."

"I know this hospital, Stover. And I've got a gun."

Another pause. Monks pictured Larrabee passing his hand over his hair.

"Where do they keep the janitor carts, all that stuff?"

"Basement," Monks said. "I'll be leaving the ER in ten to fifteen minutes, heading for the elevators. Up to the sixth floor, north wing, for five to ten more, then down to the morgue. That's in the basement, too."

The connection ended. Monks picked up the house phone and punched the extension for the morgue.

"Roman. Get rid of everybody down there. I need you alone in twenty minutes." He kept talking, trying to voice the flow chart taking shape in his mind.

When Monks came back to the ER, Jim Parrish was not in sight: presumably he was with another patient. Vernon was inside the cubicle, alone with Jephson. Monks stepped in and closed the door.

"I gave him both, Narrcan and Romazicon," Vernon said. "He's still out hard."

Monks leaned over Jephson, thinking, *What the hell?* But the answer was already coming: something Monks had not seen in more than ten years—probably chosen by someone who knew that this type of O.D. could not be brought back to consciousness for hours.

Monks said, "Barbiturates." A once popular choice for suicide. Except suicides did not typically lock themselves in car trunks.

Jephson's pulse was normal, his breathing labored but steady. A dose just short of lethal— probably deliberately, so that Monks would be forced to finish this.

He stepped outside again, motioning Vernon to follow.

"Patient was stable when you released him into my care."

"Released him?"

"This is what I asked you."

Doubt came into Vernon's eyes, but again, he nodded.

"He's mine now," Monks said. "You're no longer in any way responsible."

He walked to the ER desk. The day Charge Nurse, Helen Toner, watched his approach with guarded astonishment. He remembered that he was wearing jeans and a sweatshirt and had not shaved.

"Mrs. Toner, please admit the patient in Cubicle Four to my service on Six-North. Single room. Probable overdose, rule out coronary or stroke."

"Dr. Monks, I thought—you'd made a scheduling mistake. That is, you're not really on duty. Are you?"

"This is a slightly irregular situation. I found the man, I began his care. I'm considering myself responsible." Monks laid Jephson's wallet on the desk. "You'll find enough information here for preliminary paperwork. We'll worry about notifying relatives when he's settled."

"I'll see if they have a room."

There were personnel and patients just on the other side of the door to the waiting room. Monks leaned close and dropped his voice.

"Helen. *Find* a room. And rush the paperwork." In a normal tone, he said, "I'll take the patient up myself."

She stared. Then leaned back in her chair and said, "Yes, Doctor."

Monks pushed the gurney loaded with monitor, IV paraphernalia, and Francis Jephson, along the hall at a brisk but untroubled pace. He passed several familiar faces, maintenance workers and personnel. Others, strangers, might have been visitors or staff from another unit.

Or Naia herself.

Twenty yards behind him, Larrabee, wearing a janitor's coat, pushed a cart stacked with cleaning supplies. He paused and began dust-mopping while Monks waited for the elevator.

There were no other passengers. Monks unloaded the gurney on Six-North, a general unit for those not well enough to go home, but not requiring intensive care. Things were quiet, most patients sedated or asleep, a few chatting with visitors or watching television. He started down the hall, pausing to study his clipboard until a second elevator with Larrabee arrived.

The Nurses' Station was in an alcove midway, presided over by a pleasantly worn-looking nurse named Rose Olsen. She glanced up at his approach and blinked. It was not common to see a senior physician pushing a gurney.

Monks returned her greeting blandly and handed her the check-in forms from his clipboard.

"That's 624, Dr. Monks. It's ready. I'll help you move him."

"Rose, I'm going to leave him on the gurney a few minutes. The monitor started jumping on the way up here. I'll call you when I need you."

Monks pushed the gurney into the room and closed the door. From under the blanket he took out an evidence camera he had borrowed from the ER and positioned it on the windowsill. He took a sterile, plastic-wrapped syringe and the vial of potassium chloride from his pocket. He inserted the needle into the vial and drew liquid into the syringe, balancing both in one hand and snapping a photo at each step. He inserted the needle into the injection part of the tubing.

Then he looked down into the face of the man who had started this engine of misery.

Aloud, Monks said, "I can see why you covered up for little Robby Vandenard, way back when. Money. Status. Rubbing shoulders with the aristocracy.

"But why did you keep setting up the NGIs? The vicious thrill, like watching that video? Getting off on what Naia did, that you were too cowardly to do yourself?"

Monks held the camera against his chest with his right hand. He placed his left thumb on the syringe's plunger and snapped a photo. He snapped three more as he pushed the plunger home.

He put the syringe back in his pocket and

replugged the IV. He pulled the monitor sensor away from the skin of Jephson's chest and retaped it to the gurney's pad. The waves on the screen became a jumpy line of static. Monks took more photos.

Then he jerked open the door and called sharply, "Nurse! This patient's having PVCs."

He watched her stand in alarm and start toward him, but he stopped her with out-stretched palm, already pulling the gurney from the room.

"I'd better get him to the ICU. He can't stay here until his rhythm is stable."

He pushed the gurney past her, clandestinely wiggling the monitor cable to mimic the jumpy lines of premature ventricular contractions. Larrabee stepped aside, gaze deferentially low.

The elevator doors closed. Monks rode down, past the ICU, to the basement.

The basement corridor was empty. It was not an area that got much traffic. Except for building maintenance and supply, there was only the morgue. Monks walked slowly, until another elevator opened and Larrabee came out pushing the cart. He disappeared into the fire stairwell. Its windowed door would give a view of both sections of the L-shaped hall.

Inside the morgue, Roman was waiting, gloved, wearing smock and cap. They worked quickly, lifting Jephson onto one of the stainless steel autopsy tables, then covering him with a plasticized sheet folded down from the waist.

Roman positioned a cart with autopsy instruments—knives, bone saws, specimen jars, stainless steel bowls, and a scale—then stepped to the microwave. He took out a Tupperwarelike container and emptied its contents carefully into one of the bowls: a human heart, swimming in darkish blood. He splashed fingerfuls of blood on Jephson's chest, dabbing it around, then surrounded the area with blood-soaked towels.

Monks stood back with the camera and snapped several photos. The entire procedure had taken perhaps three minutes.

He stepped into Roman's office, picked up the house phone, and called the extension for the Emergency Room.

"Mrs. Toner, I have some terrible news. My patient, Francis Jephson, suffered what appears to be a massive coronary and died in return from the floor to the ICU. I pronounced him at 12:11 P.M. Dr. Kasmarek is performing the autopsy. Please call Admitting and see to it the death is entered on the computer bank immediately."

Silence.

Monks said, "Mrs. Toner? Was that clear?"

The faint reply came: "Right away, Doctor."

He nodded to Roman to come inside the office, and closed the door.

Roman said quietly, "How long's he out for?"

"A few more hours."

"You want me to hit him with something if he comes up?"

"If you haven't heard from me by then, get him to the police."

Monks took out the cell phone and once more called the now-familiar number that was his link to Naia.

When the tone came, he said, "It's done. The autopsy has started. I have photos, and the hospital's data bank will confirm it. Tell me where we make the exchange."

He clicked it off and waited.

Two minutes passed. Three.

The phone's chirping ring sounded. When he raised it to his ear, his palm was slippery with sweat.

"This is Monks."

"Where the fuck are you?" It was Larrabee's voice, a tense whisper.

Startled, Monks said, "In the morgue."

"You haven't left?"

"No."

"Somebody just went into the machine room. I thought it was you. I'm going to check it out."

Monks turned to Roman, gesturing to him to stay put, and strode down the hall. He looked cautiously around the corner. An empty gurney was pushed against the wall outside the door to the machine room. He trotted there on his toes, moving as quietly as he could, his hand on the pistol's butt.

The physical plant was huge, a labyrinth of pipes and machinery strung along narrow corridors to allow human passage. It was dimly lit, hot and loud with the throbbing growl of the building's pulse being pumped out through ceilings and walls. He moved a step at a time, the pistol in both sweating hands, his head turning back and forth to peer through the gloomy maze.

He inhaled, then stepped around a corner, gun ready. Several yards ahead, a man was lying on the floor facedown, his feet toward Monks.

Larrabee.

Monks turned in a circle, teeth bared. His heart was slamming with rage and fear. There was no one, no sound. Blood streamed from a gash across Larrabee's temple. Monks knelt, fingers going to a wrist. The pulse was fast but strong. Monks's hand searched for other wounds and found something protruding from the back between the shoulders.

A dart, a hypodermic syringe, the type shot from a gun.

"It's okay, buddy, we'll get you upstairs," Monks whispered. He got one arm around the torso and was rising with the weight when the edge of his vision caught the moving shadow. He started to turn, raising the pistol, but a hard crack came down on his wrist, knocking the gun from his grip, sending pain flaring through him.

Then came a *whump* and a stinging impact in his neck.

A man stepped into sight, moving fast. He was wearing a white lab coat. Monks tried to grapple, but the man shoved him aside with startling strength. Monks lurched against a wall, with a first wave of dizziness washing through him.

The man stepped over Larrabee, raising a heavy pipe wrench.

Monks lunged. His head butted into the man's abdomen and his flailing arms encircled the torso. They struggled backwards, crashing into the machinery that lined the walls. The weakness surged in Monks again. His grip loosened. He went down to a knee, then both knees, weaving and gasping for breath. The man leaned down and gripped him by the collar.

Monks looked up into a face with a thick arched nose, pitted cheeks, wiry black hair.

His own face.

He clawed at it, and felt his fingers sink into softness that was not flesh: putty or wax and thick greasy makeup.

A man disguised as Monks, but with something wrong about the eyes.

His hand was gripped with savage strength and twisted until he collapsed on the floor. He felt himself lifted easily and carried to the gurney in the hall. It was pushed with quick strides to the morgue and through the door.

Roman said, "Christ, Carroll, another one?"

The man with Monks's face raised a pistol. The *whump* sounded again. Roman staggered back. The man stepped forward and swung the barrel viciously across his face, knocking him sprawling. Then he pulled open a cadaver drawer, dumped Roman inside, and slammed it shut.

He paused at the autopsy cart with its gleaming array of surgical instruments.

Then he leaned over Monks, with a large scalpel held between their faces.

"'Emergency, huh?'" he whispered in an exaggerated twang. "'Must take good nerves.'"

The drawling voice and words touched a memory, but it was the eyes that triggered Monks's realization of where he had seen that face.

The caretaker at the Vandenards' Napa estate: an image that became superimposed in Monks's mind with another, a news photo of a man being led away in handcuffs, a much younger man, but with the same old, knowing eyes.

Monks said, pronouncing the words with great effort, "*You* picked Tommy Springkell for the program. Because he fit. Used him like a suit of clothes."

Through blurred, dimming vision, Monks watched Robby Vandenard lean over Jephson's body with busy hands, then lift out the still beating bloody heart and place it beside the decoy in a second stainless steel bowl.

16

Monks awoke with a cold gritty weight against his cheek. For a confused interval his brain tried to return to the safety of sleep, but his head was throbbing and his body ached. His left wrist felt sprained. Abruptly he remembered the blow he had taken there. Images flashed with quickening intensity through his brain: Larrabee, unconscious and bleeding; Roman in a cadaver drawer.

Both assaulted by a man disguised as himself.

He opened his eyes. He was in a room with rough stone walls, wet in patches from seeping water, that curved up to form a high-ceilinged vault. A dim even light came from wall-mounted lamps. A draft brought traces of musty, earthy scent. The cold against his cheek was the floor he lay on; the grit was sharp and unyielding, like tiny shards of glass.

Diatomaceous earth.

He struggled to sit up, fighting dizziness, and gasped at a yank around his neck. It was a leather strap, knotted to an iron rack. A horizontal row of chalk-white plaster masks was mounted along it: a fresco of men with shadowy agonized faces, held in this dark damp purgatory. A severed tether trailed beneath each. This was the place he had seen in the video of Caymas Schultz, and now he understood where he was: inside the wine cave where Katherine Vandenard had been murdered. Where Monks himself had stood outside only days before and talked to the man who had done it.

At his own place, a white mound of plaster was heaped on a board.

Monks did not need to touch it to know that it was still wet.

"You have only yourself to blame for this, Dr. Monks. If you hadn't interfered, there'd be no need for haste."

This voice was a man's, natural, without any forced high pitch or intonation now. A pale oval was moving toward Monks from the darkness, a smooth androgynous face with hairless head: the undisguised face of Robby Vandenard. The body beneath was of medium height, lithe, clothed in tight-fitting black.

"I'm going to give you something not everyone gets. A second chance. Do what I ask, and I'll let you go. You'll never hear from me again. Only—this time, I'll be here to see to it that there's no cheating."

Robby moved closer as he talked, spiraling in, with the gliding steps of a dancer or martial artist. He was holding his right hand behind his thigh, hiding what it held. Monks turned clumsily on his knees to keep him in sight, fighting his body's urge to run.

He said hoarsely, "What's the price this time? Another murder?"

Robby leaped forward, the hidden hand slashing down in a blur of speed. Monks threw himself back. The hand whispered past his ear. There was a yank at his neck. Then he was free.

Robby was smiling. He held up a knife with a wooden shaft and hooked blade. A grape-picker's knife.

"You're probably feeling a little shaky," he said. "I have a selection of stimulants and narcotics. Or perhaps you'd prefer a drink. I laid in some Finlandia vodka, especially for this occasion. A classic, isn't it? The doctor who needs a stiff shot to steady his hand?"

Monks shook his head warily.

"Take your time, then. But not too much time. Katherine and I have places to go and people to see."

Monks said, "Katherine?"

Robby's face receded back into the cave's darkness. Another light came on, in a smaller chamber that opened off the main one. This was decorated like the room of a teenaged girl, with pastel walls and furnishings. The bed in the center held several stuffed animals and dolls.

Among them lay Alison Chapley, wearing a young girl's nightgown.

Monks stood, lurching, and made his way to her. Her eyes were open, but she did not move or speak: an affect that suggested sodium pentothal or Versed. Her hair had been dyed auburn and fell straight, parted in the middle. Her eyes were lined heavily with kohl, her lipstick pale pink.

Monks's gaze rose to a photograph on a shelf, a dated professional portrait in an ornate gilt frame. Two children stood side by side. The older was a girl already taking on a woman's beauty. Long straight auburn hair, parted in the middle. Dark-lined eyes and pale lipstick.

Katherine Vandenard.

Not just the makeup, but the facial structure— eyes that sloed toward the exotic, strong cheekbones, wide mouth—made her resemblance to Alison startling.

The other child in the photo was a boy of perhaps ten, dressed in suit and tie, his fair hair curled to give an angelic appearance.

But even then, the eyes gave a hint of something much older.

"We need your help, Dr. Monks." Robby's voice came from behind him. "I was going to use

Jephson, but his hands shook like leaves. He whined that he hadn't touched an instrument in thirty years. Pitiful. I suppose it didn't help any, putting him in the car trunk with Garlick. Garlick was a mess by then.

"I considered doing it myself. It's a very simple procedure. But I just don't have that touch, the years of experience.

"Then *you* called. I thought, those steely Emergency Room nerves. Just what we need."

Robby stepped into sight again, holding a plastic, life-sized medical model of a human head. Skin and skull were transparent, revealing the convoluted sections of the brain.

"We'll use the trans-orbital method. Tried and true. It only takes a few minutes. They used to do them one right after the other, dozens in an afternoon. Insertion of a probe through the eyelids—"

He shifted the head to hold it with one hand, while the other introduced a surgical knife with a long, thin blade above the eyeball, piercing up into the central forebrain.

"Followed by severing the connection between the thalamus and frontal lobe. A twist of the wrist."

The probe slashed across.

"The vessel is cleansed, and ready for its new owner."

Robby swung the probe to point at the photograph of Katherine.

Monks stared, beginning to comprehend what Robby Vandenard intended:

A frontal lobotomy to empty the "vessel," Alison. Eliminate her personality, in the belief that he could bring back the sister he had murdered out of jealous love, almost thirty years ago.

Robby was moving again, briskly setting out a sterile tray. It held gauze, bowls of antiseptic solution, and another surgical knife still in a packet.

He help up a pair of surgical gloves.

"Size seven and a half, I believe?"

Monks said slowly, "It won't work, Robby. You'll just be destroying another life. Like Katherine's."

"I didn't *destroy* Katherine's life. I kept her from going in a wrong direction."

"What wrong direction, growing up? Becoming a normal human being?"

"She's never stopped talking to me, Monks. She told me how to feed her the cobras, to make her stronger. She brought the vessel to me. She's talking to me right now. Telling me she's very angry with you.

"When she gets angry—" the voice rose into the eerie high pitch, echoing through the vault with venomous intensity— "she becomes Naia."

Robby stepped to an alcove in the stone wall. He stood with his back turned for half a minute, leaning slightly forward, hands moving like those of a woman putting on makeup. When he turned back to Monks, his eyes were ringed in red and

dark hair streamed down his shoulders. He
advanced with the silent gliding steps. He was
holding the grape-picker's knife again.

"Everything alive consumes other life,
Monks," the high voice crooned. "Look at *her*,
and admit the truth." The knife made a hooking
gesture at Alison. "You were feeding off her all
along, lapping at her soul: her flame, her fearless-
ness, the way she put herself on the edge. When
you had your hands around her throat that night,
didn't you feel her life spilling into you? Wasn't
that what *really* scared you, the power that was so
delicious?"

Monks's hand touched his back pocket. The
razor was still there. He slid it loose, keeping it
hidden, and turned with the circling figure.

"Alison, get up!" he yelled. "Get out of here!"

Monks shuffled backwards along the iron rack.
Robby glided after him.

Then sidestepped and disappeared from sight.

Crouched, skin prickling, Monks stayed
motionless, straining to hear.

"I lived with people who understand these
things, Monks."

The voice came from above. Monks's head
jerked up so sharply a burn shot through his
neck. Robby was standing on top of the rack.

"In Africa," Robby said. "Not much fancy
modern medicine out in the bush. But cobras.
Masks. The knowledge of how death feeds life,
and how it can be used. It's as old as time."

He stepped into the air and dropped, landing silently: feet spread, poised, knife ready.

"Get up!" Monks screamed. He stumbled away, skirting around the rack's far end. His hand hooked on one of the masks. He wrenched it loose and hurled it like a discus to shatter against the wall above the bed where Alison lay.

"That," the high voice said with controlled rage, "was a mistake."

Robby lunged, driving under Monks's clumsy out-thrust arm. A hot streak of pain burned across his belly. He clasped it with his left hand, backing away, feeling the seep of slippery blood through his fingers.

Another lunge. Monks flailed out, but the quick body spun and kicked a knee out from under him. He went down heavily.

"Come on, Dr. Monks. The offer stands. A couple of bandages and a shot of Demerol and you'll be fine. *I* don't hold grudges."

Monks got to his feet and ran blindly, staggering, colliding with the walls, deafened by his own shrieking breath. Another hot slice flared across his back. He hit the stone floor on hands and knees, the razor flying from his hand and skittering across the floor.

He screamed, *"You can't empty out a human being like a jar and fill it up with somebody who's dead."*

Monks dragged himself a little further and lay still, his cheek again on the stone, cool and comforting now. He was aware of his blood slipping away.

The pain seeped away with it, and an image appeared in his mind, of a day almost two decades earlier, at the beach at Point Reyes. Crystal blue sky, hot sun and fresh breeze, miles of pristine sand. His young wife with their son and daughter, playing in the surf: the perfect family, in a life and world that seemed as fresh as they themselves.

"All right, Monks, I'll have to do it myself after all," the voice said. It sounded very far away. "But I'll need some practice first. Let's see, where shall I start? *I* know."

Monks felt a hand on his neck, then the pressure of a knee across the small of his back, the full weight of a man coming to rest. Something sharp hooked into the flesh at the inside tendon behind his right knee.

In that instant of pause, there came a sound that he could feel: a *tchhh*, like a knife slicing into a slab of meat.

A splash of warm liquid hit his neck and face. The weight on his body lessened, then lifted.

Monks forced his eyes to open. Robby Vandenard was on his knees, swaying, both hands clasping the left side of his throat. Blood was pumping between his fingers with the quick rhythm of pulse.

Behind him, Alison stood, with the razor in her hand.

It fell from her fingers. As if it had held invisible puppet strings that supported him, Robby dropped back to his haunches, then sagged again.

He settled beside Monks like a shy lover, his face only a few inches away. Blood pulsed from the gaping slash across his carotid artery. Monks's hand moved of itself to compress the wound, but then stopped, his mind knowing it was hopeless. He felt a sensation he knew all too well, of a life leaving, with coldness where it had been.

But this coldness lingered, becoming a *something*. It swiftly gathered power, like an iron talon closing around his being, crushing his breath. Terror struck him that it was Robby, trying to take Monks with him. Monks rolled away, fighting to stay conscious, to escape.

His blurred vision caught the white-clad figure of Alison, returning from across the room, holding something in her hands.

The heaped mound of wet plaster from the iron rack.

She knelt over Robby, moving without haste, gazing down without expression into his face. She dipped a finger into the blood that had pooled in the hollow of his neck, raised it to her face, and circled both her eyes.

Robby's mouth twitched to form a word, a name, that Monks could not quite hear but understood without question.

Katherine.

His eyes softened, became the eyes of a boy

again. Then whoever was looking out through them began to fade.

Monks watched her smooth the plaster in handfuls over Robby's face.

The icy fury slipped out of him, like poison drawn from a snakebite, and he allowed himself to fall into a rest that was safe.

17

Monks drove the Bronco up the narrow road to his house in midafternoon, feeling weary but good. He had finished a twelve-hour shift in Mercy Hospital's Emergency Room, and now had five days of freedom ahead. It was April, the winter rains over and the sun warming the earth: perfect weather for a leisurely canoe trip on Tomales Bay, with thick salami and Gruyère sandwiches and iced-down bottles of Moretti beer.

He pulled over at his mailbox to retrieve the usual accumulation of medical journals and junk. The door was jammed tightly shut. Dark thoughts toward the mail carrier passed through his mind. He yanked at the stubborn latch, trying to remember the amount of the Christmas bonus he had ponied up.

When the door gave, he had just enough time to register skinned knuckles and real annoyance. Then it came home to him that something was clawing its way up the bare flesh of his forearm.

Frozen, he stared. It was a rat, with small insane eyes and bared teeth, lunging toward his face.

Monks's paralysis ended at the same instant the rat seemed to realize that it was heading toward confrontation rather than escape, somewhere around the elbow. He yelled and flailed his arm as if it was on fire. The rat leaped free. His last glimpse was of it slithering through the thick duff of redwood needles and oak leaves blanketing the earth, looking more like a reptile than a mammal, working its way deeper until only its pink naked tail remained.

Monks turned warily back to the mailbox and pulled free its contents. Magazines and envelopes came out in festoons of confetti and rat shit.

He drove uphill to the house, shaking with anger and fear. He walked straight to his safe and took out the shotgun.

Then he exhaled and put it back, realizing that he was starting to feel sorry for the rat. It had not locked itself into the mailbox, and could hardly be blamed for trying to rip the skin off something many times its size, reaching into its trap.

He dutifully checked rooms and closets. No one appeared to have been inside. The usual accumulation of dust seemed undisturbed.

So. The message seemed clear enough. Someone considered him to be a rat, and had, so to
speak, put teeth in it.

He picked up a phone and called the local post
office. It took him over a minute to get through a
phone tree. The woman who answered sounded
young, and so languid that Monks tentatively
diagnosed vapors. He gave his name and address,
and added:

"I came home today and found a rat in my
mailbox."

"A rat?"

"Correct."

The next pause lengthened. Monks said help-
fully, "R-A-T."

"Was it, like, packaged? I mean, was there
postage?"

"No."

"Then I don't think it was us, sir."

"Am I right that it's a federal offense to put an
object without postage into a mailbox?"

Her voice took on a tone of formality. "Do you
wish to file a complaint?"

"Will someone come out and investigate if I
do?"

Pause. "You'd have to call the police about
that."

"If I call the police, they'll say a mailbox is federal property and out of their jurisdiction. I speak
from experience, you see," he said, feeling it getting away from him, knowing there was no point

in taking this out on a clerk. "Every so often it gets bashed in by adolescent boys, and whoever I complain to tells me it's someone else's problem. Meaning, of course, mine."

"I'm sorry, sir," she said, now with the patient weariness of dealing with a crank.

"Have you ever heard of Synanon House, Miss?"

"Sin what?"

He envisioned her sitting up sharply, pushing an alarm button or starting a tape recorder, whatever they did with calls that threatened to turn obscene.

"Long story," Monks said. "Someone did the same thing, only with a rattlesnake. It almost killed a man."

Silence.

"Vandalism is one thing," Monks said, "but a live rat—I thought," and, conscious that he had lost the battle, he finished weakly, "someone might be concerned. "

He placed the phone in its cradle.

When he got to the kitchen, the cats were waiting.

"There's a rodent outside calling you guys pussies," Monks said.

He was met with stony stares and yawns. Then he remembered: these were cats that had faced down a cobra. A rat was far beneath their dignity. He opened two cans of Kultured Kat turkey and giblets, feeling vaguely that the fowl was appropriate, and divided it up.

Then he took out the Finlandia. It smoked as it poured over the ice cubes. He touched it with fresh lemon, drank it, and made another. He took this one out to the deck and stood at the railing, watching the light on the Pacific horizon, remembering back the several months, to cobras.

Stover Larrabee and Roman Kasmarek had come out damaged but alive, the first with a severe concussion and the second with a fractured cheekbone. They had been discovered and treated by a sharp young doc named Vernon Dickhaut, who had gone looking for Monks after the bizarre incidents in the hospital that day.

Robby Vandenard's tracks had been traced by the police as far as was possible. He had been no fool about practicalities: had hidden large sums of money in numbered overseas accounts, bought property under false identities, hacked his way into illegal computer links that included LEIN and NCIC law enforcement networks. The chances of finding him again, with Alison made surgically docile and the likelihood of plastic surgery, would have been remote.

There had been much speculation about his psychology. Incestuous urges toward his sister, certainly. Rationalization of severe cognitive dissonance, a refusal to accept the fact that he had murdered her, resulting in a belief that she still lived within him. Reinforcement of this by assuming her persona and repeatedly avenging her death, in a violent form of belated mastery.

The belief that by killing, he could add the "cobras" to her strength, like horses to a chariot. Which finally resulted in her signaling him that she was ready to return: into the flesh of Alison Chapley.

But the person who knew the most about it took his secrets with him when he died on the autopsy table in Mercy Hospital. Several more videos of the NGIs being stalked and killed had been found hidden in Jephson's house. No other records had turned up to indicate whether he was moved by threat, by vicarious pleasure in the murder of men he had feared, or by something else entirely. Monks had revised his opinion again about Jephson's rattlesnake bite, guessing that it had been brought about by Robby, in an early move to terrorize the man he would continue to dominate for three more decades. Or perhaps it was a declaration of passion.

As for Alison, she was gone: back to the East Coast, a long vacation, and a slow segue into private practice, away from the violent men who had been her fascination. Monks had received an occasional postcard from her, and sent the same back.

He walked inside and took from his desk the last card he had received. It was a painting by Caspar David Friedrich, of a distant solitary figure standing on a beach, overwhelmed by the stormy sky and choppy ocean behind him. It was titled *The Monk at the Sea*. There was no message on it, only her signature. He surmised that it was the end of what could hardly have been called a correspondence.

He did not think of her as having deceived him. He understood that she had been driven by a need more powerful than the ties that drew her to him. And that that need of hers had been fulfilled, the deep question in her being, that answered. It was too private for her to share—or perhaps, to be reminded of—and so she had put distance between them.

But from his own side, there was a chillier part to it. He could not entirely shake the sense that for those few instants, while he had watched her paint her eyes and smooth the death mask over Robby's face, it *had* happened:

Katherine Vandenard—Naia—had touched her.

He poured another drink and started looking through his files, trying to spot the enraged malpractitioner who wanted revenge on Monks for ratting him off.

Don't Miss These Other Acclaimed Thrillers by

JAMES GRIPPANDO

FOUND MONEY
0-06-109762-4/$6.99 US/$9.99 Can
"Greed, family secrets, and the dangers of getting
what you wish for. . . . A wild ride."
Publishers Weekly

THE PARDON
0-06-109286-X/$6.99 US/$9.99 Can
"Powerful . . . I read *The Pardon* in one sitting—
one exciting night of thrills and chills."
James Patterson

THE INFORMANT
0-06-101220-3/$6.50 US/$8.50 Can
"A thoroughly convincing edge-of-your-seat thriller."
John Douglas, bestselling author of *Mind Hunter*

THE ABDUCTION
0-06-109748-9/$6.99 US/$8.99 Can
"Nonstop plot surprises. . . .
One of the year's better thrillers."
San Francisco Examiner

Available Now in Hardcover

UNDER COVER OF DARKNESS
0-06-019240-2/$25.00 US/$37.95 Can